2B

Determined

2B
Determined

by **Cindy Neuschwander**
illustrations by **Emily Tetri**

Chocolate Puddle Press
California • USA

Special thanks to:
Aimee Jackson, who orchestrated this project
Eric Braun, my amazing and insightful editor
Michelle Lee Lagerroos, book designer extraordinaire
Emily Tetri, who brought my characters to life

Text and artwork copyright © 2023 Cindy Neuschwander
Illustrations by Emily Tetri
Design by Michelle Lee Lagerroos
Edited by Eric Braun
All rights reserved.

Chocolate Puddle Press
cindy@chocolatepuddlepress.com
chocolatepuddlepress.com
California, USA

Printed and bound in the United States of America
First Edition
10 9 8 7 6 5 4 3 2 1
LCCN 2023904630
ISBN 979-8-218-17279-4

book bridge press

This book was proudly produced by Book Bridge Press.
www.bookbridgepress.com

For Annika and Scott
—C. N.

To Fin and Waffle who were a
couple of good sniff detectives
—E. T.

New Home

BLAM! Aroma bombs exploded inside my nose. Conducting a stealthy sniff-over, I detected the rich, greasy scents of barbecue ribs on a napkin stuffed in a pocket. Letting my nose linger, I could also smell earthy garden compost near some knees and cheesy toe fungus inside a shoe. These were my kind of humans.

I was at the front desk of the dog shelter, eagerly straining to leave with this couple who had chosen to adopt . . . me!

Goodbye, BARC. Goodbye, volunteers. Goodbye, kennel run. Hello, new life!

I eagerly jumped into the back seat of a fancy new car and nose-smudged the window as we drove away. This was going to be great!

"Here, Prince," my new man-owner called when we arrived at my home. "Behold! Your kingdom."

He wasn't kidding.

In a fenced side yard was a doghouse that looked like a miniature castle. Inside, a puffy dog cushion awaited me like a throne for a real prince.

"We're making the world a better place, adopting a stray like you," my new man-owner said proudly.

"With all the comforts a dog could want, Prince," added my new lady-owner. "You're a lucky, lucky boy!" She patted me lightly on the head. Then the two of them closed the kennel run gate and left.

Meaty mutt meals! I thought. *This is double-dog fantabulous!*

And it was—for a hot ten minutes. But we dogs are social by nature. It means we like company and that, I discovered, was the one thing missing in my new realm. Sure, I got a short walk some mornings and I was fed twice a day, but other than that it was me, myself, and I. Where was the roaring fireplace, me curled at my humans' feet? Where were the slippers I would retrieve for them each evening?

Time to take things into my own paws, I thought after I had spent a few lonely days pacing the length and width of my run. I needed to show them what makes a dog happy. I was sure it would make them happy too.

I eyed the fence around my run. Definitely jumpable. I easily sailed over the gate and trotted out onto the manicured front yard.

Gotta dig that! I thought, diving into some gorgeous flower beds. Mmmm! They smelled like freshly laundered sheets. Plus the cool moist dirt felt so good on the paws. Much better than my concrete slab. I loped around the house, looking for a way in.

At the back, I noticed an open window, covered only by a screen.

"Easy-peasy!" I woofed, dive-bombing through it. The screen tore like a soggy Kleenex and I landed on a cool granite countertop. Sliding along, I accidentally collided with a tall glass vase filled with sun-yellow tulips. Fortunately, I came to a stop before the counter ended.

I wish I could say the same for the flowers. *CRASH!* They and their vase ended up in parts and petals on the tiled kitchen floor. Neatly arranged place mats on the breakfast table looked like a smart way to cover up the mess.

I leaped from the counter to the table, sticking the landing. *Floop, floop, floop.* I tossed the place mats onto

the floor like Frisbees. They did a nice job of hiding the incriminating evidence once known as the flower vase.

"*Rowrff! Rowrff?*" My deep barks echoed through the house. "Anybody here?"

Making myself at home, I moved down hallways, into bedrooms, and up and down staircases searching for my new family. I'd never been in a place this fancy before.

Other than the kitchen, this house was so clean specks of dust needed to ask for permission to land. I'd worked up a thirst getting inside, so I was pleased to discover a toilet bowl brimming with clear, fresh water. After a few splashy slurps, I rubbed my drippy muzzle on the full roll of toilet paper. It popped off its holder and unwound down the hall.

I eagerly followed it like a cat after a yarn ball. It ran out of steam near an office. I stepped inside. On an ornately carved wooden desk sat a computer and a pair of glasses.

The glasses smelled like my new man-owner. Pulling them onto the floor, I tenderly licked and nibbled at them, thanking him for adopting me.

Crunch!

In my enthusiasm, I bent the frames and one lens popped out. Leaving them behind, I turned my attention to further discoveries.

I cruised into what smelled like my owners' bedroom. There were the slippers. And they were tender, tasty leather to boot. After a satisfying chew fest, I reluctantly moved on, enjoying a sniff party in the laundry room. Let me tell you, there were some great whiffs in there. The dirty T-shirts and underwear gave off meaty, salty smells. I happily flung them everywhere and even ate a sock or two. But no worries. Everything always comes out well in the end, if you know what I mean.

I stood still and barked once more. *"Rowrff!"* But it was so quiet I could hear myself shedding. No one here but me, that was for sure. I'd just have to wait until they got home.

Trotting into the living room, I looked around for the fireplace. But there wasn't one. There would be no snoozing in front of crackling logs or glowing embers. A nap on a comfy-looking leather couch would have to do instead. As I jumped onto the deliciously soft sofa, I stepped on a small box.

Poof!

A friendly blaze appeared on the big-screen TV across from me. Not quite what I had in mind but . . . better than nothing. I slid into a satisfied slumber.

I was awakened later by voices. My new family was arriving home. I hurried to greet them, my tail wagging into a furry blur.

"Oh no!" screamed my new lady-owner, looking around at my messes.

"What the . . . !" yelled my new man-owner.

"This dog has got to go!" they both chimed in.

And so I did.

Without ever learning their names, I went back to The BARC, my home sweet dog-shelter home.

Dog Days of Summer

BARC stands for **B**est-ever **A**doption **R**esidence for **C**anines. It's staffed with kind-hearted, well-meaning volunteers who keep our kennel runs clean and feed us kibble regularly. They say it's the best dog shelter in all of Jacksonville, North Carolina.

The folks who run our shelter think the blazing hot days of July is the perfect time to hold their annual *Dog Days of Summer Canine Adoption Event*. It could be because our lobby is air-conditioned and people come in for the coolness. Or maybe they think the snappy name brings attention to us stray dogs and our homeless plight. Who knows?

The goal is to get us out the front doors of the shelter and into the embracing arms of loving forever-families. The BARC has been successful at it over the years, for the most part. I'm the other part—the part that hasn't been so successful. I've been returned there more times than borrowed books to a library.

Panting on the cool concrete floor, I felt overheated in the shaggy mottled coat I couldn't remove. My long legs sprawled every which way. I could hear the not-so-distant rumbling of the highway through a window high above me. Shiny helium balloons in the shapes of paws and biscuits bobbed about cheerfully in the lobby.

A young woman in a floppy sundress and sandals flounced past the decorations and into the kennel runs. I sat up hopefully, giving her my widest dog smile and softest brown-eyed look. *Choose me!* I thought.

"Ooooh!" she squealed. "You're the one! I adore you!" But she had stopped in front of the cage directly across from mine. A sturdy black puppy looked through the wire at her, his chocolate-drop eyes melting her heart.

"You and I are going places together, Little Buddy," she cooed. Opening his cage, she scooped him up and nuzzled that snuggly ball of fur. She snapped a selfie of the two of them with her phone and strode out to the adoption desk.

A few minutes and a few forms later, lucky Little Buddy was out the door with his loving human.

And why exactly can't I find that special forever-person? I wondered. *What's wrong with me?*

Once I had been as lucky as Little Buddy, I remembered. Long ago, a young woman walked through these very kennel runs, looking at each of us. She stopped suddenly in front of my cage and knelt down. She wore baggy black-and-white checked pants and a white jacket that buttoned up to her neck. Her curly dark-brown hair was piled up in a messy bun.

"Oh, sweet one!" she said to me softly, putting her fingers through the wires.

No, I thought. *You are the sweet one!* Her scent was delicious: a combination of many excellent smells. She would teach me all their names: osso buco, calamari, potato gnocchi, apricot tart, and my all-time favorite smell on her, orange creamsicle. I gently licked her fingers.

"Such a smoochie pooch!" she murmured tenderly.

Her name was Dragana, which I found out later meant *beautiful* in her native language. And she *was* beautiful. She took me home that day and, for a while, our lives together were beautiful too.

I was pulled out of my pleasant reverie by the not-so-quiet snuffling of my new next-door neighbor. He had arrived earlier in the morning. Glancing into cage 3-B,

I noticed an older basset hound inspecting his run. He stopped next to our shared wire wall. We did a nose-to-butt sniff introduction, leaning side to side against the fencing.

"Hello," he said. "My name is Maurice. Judging by your smells, you appear to be an earnest but lonely four-year-old mixed breed dog who ate lamb and rice kibble for your last meal. Perhaps you recently eliminated some soiled athletic socks."

"Call me 2B," I responded.

The already wrinkly skin on his forehead wrinkled even more deeply. "You are named after your kennel run number?"

"I've probably had almost as many names as the number of people who live around here," I answered. "But, since I always seem to end up back here, 2B just stuck."

He gave me a sympathetic look. "Oh! Lots of homes that did not work out?"

"Yeah, something like that," I said. "What's your story?"

"I am an orphaned immigrant," he said sorrowfully.

"Sounds sad," I responded. "Tell me more."

"Ah," sighed Maurice. "I was adopted as a puppy by a wonderful man, Phillipe Babineux. He was an accomplished chef from a famous restaurant in Paris. He took several trips to the United States when he was a young man and fell in love with this place. A few years ago, we packed up and moved here. Together we opened a small restaurant: Bistro Babineux.

"Sadly, he passed away a few days ago. He has only a sister, Perline, and she lives in France. I am sure she will be coming to bring me home soon. In the meantime I reside at The BARC, just as you do."

"I was once owned by a cooking school student," I told him.

"Then you know a thing or two about fine dining, yes?" he asked.

"A bit," I grunted. And with that, I turned around in a circle a few times, plopped down, and went to sleep.

If Wishes Were Biscuits

"**M**orning, 2B," said the kennel keeper. "Here's your breakfast." And with a quick pat on my head he was down the row, feeding Maurice and the other residents.

I stared moodily at my bowl. The BARC was strangely quiet after so many dogs were adopted yesterday. But, like usual, I was still here.

Maurice looked at me through the wire wall that separated our enclosures.

"A dollop of crème frâiche would do much to enliven the meal," he said. "Dry dog food is so predictable."

"Mmm," I agreed. I actually knew about crème frâiche, that soury whipped cream often seen on French desserts. Dragana had always made her own, and I sometimes got the leftovers from the bowl. But that was then and now was now.

Then Maurice began to whimper.

I stared at him. "You OK?"

"So sorry," he said. "Phillipe and I used to sit together every evening after the Bistro closed. We would enjoy steak tartare and pommes frites while we considered the events of the day. Solitary eating is so . . . lonely."

I nosed my bowl over toward the wire wall. "So let's be dining companions."

That perked up Maurice considerably. He pushed his bowl over, and together we crunched through our kibble.

After a deep drink from our water buckets, we lay down and began to pass the time.

"Do you like living here, 2B?"

"It's a roof over my head," I said. "The people are kind, but like most dogs, I'd wish for more."

"If you could wish for anything," Maurice asked me, "what would it be?"

"I don't know," I answered vaguely. "A permanent one-way ticket out of here, I guess."

"Now that Phillipe is gone, I would wish to be back home in Paris at the restaurant with Perline," he said emphatically.

I couldn't tell Maurice, or anyone, that my true deepest wish was to be with Dragana again. But my wonderful culinary academy student had given me away. She hadn't really wanted me, not permanently. It was all ancient history, anyway. My best bet was someone else. So far, I hadn't found that person.

"Do you believe in the Furry DogMother, 2B?"

"Never heard of her," I answered. "Is she anything like that fairy godmother lady in Cinderella?" I'd lived with a few families with little kids so I knew that story.

"Yes," he said. "In France, we dogs send our most special and secret wishes to her. Why not try it? It cannot hurt, and it might help."

I snorted. "If wishes were dog biscuits, I'd have a lifetime supply of Milk-Bones by now."

But Maurice had already nodded off for a morning nap. He snored loudly.

For some reason, though, his words itched at me like sand fleas at the beach. Why not try it?

"OK, Furry DogMother, whoever and wherever you are," I whispered. "I wish someone would adopt me. And like that Little Buddy pup yesterday, it would be nice to be adored."

Then I, too, fell asleep.

Adopted Again

A short while later I was awakened by footsteps and voices coming down our hallway. I could smell the gentle soapy scent of the kennel keeper and bitter, sharp scents from two unidentified humans.

"Our population is low right now," the kennel keeper was saying. "We had a very successful adoption event yesterday, but there are still a few wonderful dogs to choose from. Take your time. You can contact me at the desk."

He left the couple in the runs. I could hear them talking as they moved down the hallway.

"Doreen? This is crazy. You've been styling people's hair for years, and we spent all that money turning our motor home into a mobile hair salon. And now you want to switch to dogs?"

"Dwayne, calm down. You were there yesterday when that lady whose hair I permed asked me to groom her dog for that show. She paid big bucks for the job."

"True," Dwayne answered. "She did seem happy about it. Plus she promised to tell all her dog show friends about you."

"So let's find ourselves a walking pooch advertisement, and we'll rake in tons of dough."

"OK, OK," said Dwayne. "If you think you can pull in some of the green stuff by styling dogs, getting a mutt to strut your skills at the dog show is a great idea. And, these dogs only cost ten bucks! What looks good?"

"This dog seems kinda droopy, and his hair is too short."

She was referring to Maurice, my new basset hound neighbor. They trudged down the row, away from us and back again, stopping and looking and moving on.

"We may have to nix this idea, Dwayne," said Doreen. "I don't really see much."

"Even if we can't find a dog," answered Dwayne, "I changed the sign on the motor home from *Doos by Doreen* to *Dogs by Doreen*. That'll be a big advertisement. I just painted a hook at the bottom of the second *o* and made it into a *g*." He sounded quite proud of his cleverness.

My run is so near the front, people tend to miss me in their rush to look at other dogs. As the couple made their way back to the lobby, Doreen stopped at my kennel.

"Check out this mutt. He's got quite a coat."

We stood staring at each other through the cage door, my dog grin big enough to split my face. I was bowled over when Dwayne said to the kennel keeper, "We'd like this one." Was it Maurice's Furry DogMother or my marvelous charms? It didn't matter . . . I would take it!

As she filled in the adoption forms, Doreen asked, "What's his name?"

"2B," answered the keeper.

"Well, 2B, nice to meet you," Dwayne said. He slipped an old rope over my head, and we headed out of The BARC. I glanced back at Maurice and wagged my tail goodbye.

Another day, another dog home, I thought. And this time, I intended to make it permanent.

We made our way through the parking lot and into their run-down RV. Then we rumbled out onto Highway 27. Soon we turned off onto a gravel road.

The PoodlePalooza

There were huge billboards everywhere along the way, with pictures of fancy dogs all over them.

A gate attendant dressed in a poodle skirt greeted us. "Welcome! Motor home parking is off to the left.

We found a spot, pulled in, and hooked up to water and power. While Doreen got ready to practice her newly found grooming skills on me, Dwayne logged onto the internet to find out more about the PoodlePalooza.

"This is quite a big deal," he told Doreen as she gathered towels and shampoo. "There are Best of Breed competitions, exhibits, races, and cash prizes."

"You keep reading up on it while I work on 2B," she responded. "Once I'm finished, we'll take a stroll around the show with him to drum up business."

She turned on the radio and a deep, velvety voice said, "This is your host Warm Storm with an afternoon of smooth jazz." Rich, complicated notes slipped and slid through the motor home. Everything here was tight and compact. Cubbyholes and tiny cabinets lined the walls. The place reminded me of a large sailboat I had briefly lived on. At least I wouldn't get seasick this time. That had been a deal breaker with the boat owner. She didn't like cleaning up dog barf.

With me relaxing, Doreen started in on the challenge that was my coat. Long, shaggy, and uncombed, it was way overdue for some cleaning up. By now, the music had lulled me into a pleasant mutt memory.

Dragana and I were in her tiny apartment. She loved jazz, and it played softly in the background. It was evening, and she was stirring a sauce. She cooked during the day as well at the Culinary Academy, where she was learning to be a chef.

She bent over with a spoonful. *Wiff.* I sucked in the complicated aromas through my two large nostrils.

Pahfff. Then I snorted them out through my nose slits. We dogs are fortunate to have these. After exhaling, that air swirls around our sniffers, gathering up even more smell molecules that stick to our big, moist, spongy noses. All these odors make their way to a special upper chamber in our snouts, where they are stored, analyzed, and sent to our brains.

And our scent memory is totally unbeatable. We never forget an aroma. The Big Guy in the Sky sure knew what He was doing when He designed our sniffers!

"Does it smell completely delicious, Wonder Nose?" she had asked me. "I wish I could figure out fragrances half as well as you. What more should I add?"

I plucked a packet of saffron out of the spice drawer and placed it at her feet. Its earthy, floral scent would make her sauce a big hit!

An acrid stench snapped me back to my present situation.

Pahffff! I snorted and did a full body shake, knocking a huge bucket of small hair curlers across the motor home.

"2B!" exclaimed Doreen, a big brush in her hand. "Look what you've done! Sit still while I finish combing out your perm."

"Give him a break," said Dwayne. "You've been working on that dog for over two hours."

I glanced into Doreen's salon mirror. What I saw shocked me. I was a massive cloud of fluffy white fur.

"The dye job worked real well," Doreen said proudly. "If I didn't know any better, I would bet the house he was a poodle."

"We should take the poor guy for a walk," Dwayne said.

"Let me style his coat, first," Doreen answered.

I noticed several pictures of very sculpted poodles taped around the mirror. Surely she wasn't planning on doing that to me?

BZZZZ went the electric clippers. A bit here, a bit there. I was rapidly turning into a collection of large pom-poms.

"All done!" announced Doreen, after spritzing me with hair spray. "Now, let's get you out and mingling with all those potential canine customers!"

The New and Improved 2B

I eagerly bounded out of the motor home and into a seemingly endless ocean of dogs and their handlers. I braced myself to be the butt of canine wisecracks. But to my surprise, it was just the opposite.

Wherever we walked, dogs and owners parted like we were royalty and stood respectfully on either side of us. *Ooohs* and *ahhhs* could be heard all around. People clamored to take pictures of me.

"Oh! Gorgeous!" exclaimed one woman. "Absolutely gorgeous!"

"I agree," said a man with two dogs. "He's one to watch, for sure."

"That one's going to take top honors, I'll wager," said another.

Was this what it felt like to be adored? *Not bad*, I thought. *Not bad at all*. Maybe Maurice's Furry DogMother wish was working. Who knew? If I wasn't in such a hurry to take a pee, I would have stuck around for more adoring. It felt good after so much ignoring.

Soon we arrived at a Canine Relief Area. That's a fancy way of saying Dog Toilets. These places are also Pup Post Offices. It's here dogs send pee-mails and poop packages to each other. Owners and handlers stay outside the large dirt enclosures, allowing us dogs to do our business.

We read with our noses. I snuffled up nervous and nattery news.

"Why can't those blasted St. Bernoodles control their drooling?"

"I'm not allowed to sit before I go in the ring because it will flatten my fanny fluff."

"Can't we just be dogs? Hair spray is so wrong!"

As I sniffed through them, I added uplifting pee-mails of my own such as, *"Every dog has its day. This could be your special one!"*

Moving on to yet another bush, I passed by a tiny poohuahua squatting in a corner.

"Hey, Snowball," he growled aggressively. "Keep your distance."

"Chill, little guy, chill," I responded, surprised by his rudeness.

"Little guy? Nobody insults Tall Paul," he snarled, hurling his diminutive body at me.

Tall Paul? I thought as I took off running. *That dude's got the shortest legs I've ever seen.*

I leaped over the Canine Relief Area fence. Surprisingly, he made it over too, nipping at my well-coiffed tail. I turned on my afterburners and sprinted, but I couldn't shake him.

CRASH! We ran right through the middle of the Dalmoodle Drill Team competition.

"Sorry!" I huffed, plowing into some of the marchers. One team went tumbling, their rhythm and routine definitely disturbed.

Judges rushed toward us, blowing whistles and shouting, "Grab those dogs!"

Glancing back, I could see Tall Paul, the judges, some dalmoodles, and in the distance Doreen, all chasing after me. On I barreled, picking up steam. So did my pursuers.

Dancing Dogfish! I thought. *Are those roller sleds dead ahead?*

They were, with teams of puskeys racing through a slalom course. I jumped aboard one and hung on around the sharp turns, feeling like a gladiator in a runaway chariot. Of course I hadn't battled anyone. Quite the opposite:

I had run from a fight. Nevertheless, crowds were cheering the racers and, as it turned out, me too. I leaped off the sled as it made a pass by the motorhome parking lot.

"2B!" yelled Doreen, puffing when she arrived. "Bad dog! Look at the mess you've made. We'll be drummed out of here for your poor behavior!"

My poor behavior? I'd been minding my own business when I was threatened by that crazy poohuahua, Tall Paul. My entire opinion of him could honestly be summed up in the first syllable of his breed name: Poo.

But Doreen was wrong. News spread fast here, and soon humans and dogs were jostling around us.

"You've got *some* grooming skills, Doreen!" said a big man. "If your dog can go through a chase like that and still look great, then we want what he's got. Sign us up for a session, and hang the cost!"

Did they adore *me* . . . or was it just the hair styling?

In the midst of all of this, Dwayne came striding back waving a handful of paper numbers.

Show Dog

"I've entered 2B in the dog show! They've got cash prizes!" he announced. "He's in the Poodle Plus division."

At last! This would be the way to prove how adorable and valuable I was. Bring on that show ring! Watch out, judges! Comin' right at you!

"Sounds great, Dwayne," mumbled Doreen. She was very busy scheduling hair appointments for her many eager customers. Did she even care?

Dwayne and I found an empty ring and we walked and ran around it, just like he had learned on the internet.

For a large, paunchy man, Dwayne was surprisingly light on his feet. He deftly took me through my paces several times until it felt like we were a team. We moved well together.

As our late afternoon competition time slot neared, Dwayne took me back to the motor home for a hair touch-up. Doreen was frazzled, but she squeezed me into her busy schedule. Dwayne changed into a coat and tie.

"Whoa!" she exclaimed. "What's gotten into you, Mr. Fancy Pants?"

"Handlers have to dress up," he explained, rubber banding a number onto his jacket sleeve.

And out we went to the ring. Crowds were thick around the flagged-in fencing. Like a golf competition I'd once seen on TV, the onlookers were respectfully quiet.

Trit, trit, trit. Around the show ring we glided. I stood patiently as the judge examined my teeth and eyes. I lined up with the other dogs while the judge carefully watched us.

"2B," announced the judge, pointing directly at me. "Second place. Congratulations. You qualify for the Best of Breeds competition tomorrow."

He handed Dwayne a ribbon, which he slipped into his jacket pocket. My first-ever award. I felt so proud of my efforts. I was sure Doreen and Dwayne would be proud too.

As we returned to the motor home, I suddenly felt dog-tired.

"*Rrrawwwl*," I yawned.

It had been a long day for me, being both an adored hair model and a second-place winner in my division.

"We made a boatload of cash today, Dwayne," Doreen proudly informed him.

"Way to go!" Dwayne replied. "2B didn't win any money in the ring yet, but he's in another round tomorrow."

"Well," Doreen said. "There's no such thing as a free lunch around here! I hope he contributes some cash. He's gotta pay for his dog food, ya know."

Dwayne nodded and handed her some brochures. "Here's a bunch of other events we can attend. You can groom tons of dogs."

"Great!" said Doreen. "Let's get to as many of these as we can."

They put their heads together and started mapping out their new life in the traveling circus of dog shows while I looked for a place to curl up and sleep. The bathroom rug was a tad small, but it worked. As I lay down, I hoped Dwayne would remember my ribbon in his pocket. I was sure they would want to hang it in a place of honor on their motor home wall.

That night I dreamed I was gliding around the show ring . . .

"First place," the judge says. *He hands Dwayne a huge trophy.*

"Oh, 2B!" Dwayne gushes. "Doreen and I are so proud of you. We truly adore you! You'll be ours forever!"

The Finals

The next day was more of the same. There were long lines at the motor home for grooming touch-ups for the show dogs. Dwayne and I kept out of the way by walking through the exhibits.

"These are real nice collars," he said, stopping at one booth. "Might make you really shine this evening." Then he looked at the price and said, "On second thought, the one you have should be fine."

The Best of Breeds round contained twenty dogs. The showing was in the large indoor arena at the fairgrounds. It was packed with people.

As the announcer read off our names, we bounded out into an echo chamber of applause to our place in the ring. "Poodle Plus consolation finalist 2B, accompanied by his handler and owner, Mr. Dwayne Dorkins."

How proud I was to hear the word *owner*!

"Hey, Snowball," growled a voice next to me.

I looked over and saw Tall Paul, winner of the Poohuahua division. He wore a jeweled collar that shimmered in the spotlights. His owner/handler was a slim, well-dressed woman. She had a delicate, elegant smell about her.

Beside her, Dwayne looked like a big teddy bear stuffed into a too-small suit. I wore my old nylon BARC collar. We all stood in a line while the judge examined each of us.

When our turn came, Dwayne and I were magic in the ring. We moved together so well, it looked like we were a pair from a Hollywood dance competition.

My only worry was a huge, unbearable itch I had during our last pass. I sat down, gave a quick but accurate scratch, and popped up again. I wasn't sure the judges had even noticed.

We waited with the rest of the competitors as the judges conferred and announced their decisions. "The Best in Show award goes to poohuahua Tall Paul and his owner/handler Amanda Puant."

Amanda Puant stepped forward graciously to accept her prize as wild applause crashed through the arena like a big wave surfer's dream swell.

"Congratulations," said the head judge. He handed her a trophy and a slender, jeweled collar for Tall Paul. A cardboard cutout of a check for $1,000 was also presented to the winners.

"Thank you," she said. Then, eyeing me, she added, "Perhaps next year you might want to highlight fewer dog categories. Isn't Poodle Plus a new division? I'm not sure it adds much to the show."

Ouch. Thanks, lady.

"Eleventh place, Doreen," Dwayne announced when we arrived back awhile later. I proudly wore the violet award ribbon on my collar. Doreen had stayed behind cleaning up from all her grooming appointments.

"That's nice," she remarked vacantly. "Did I mention we made a truckload of money today? Even better than yesterday's haul."

"We're on our way!" he cheered.

"Yep," she agreed. "I think I've established my reputation." She looked at me kind of strangely. "We can probably lighten our load tomorrow, if ya know what I mean."

The next morning Dwayne opened the door and said, "OK, Big Guy. Out you go."

I hopped out eagerly, sniffing around and doing my doggie business by a tree down the way, wondering where our next show would be.

This is going to be great! I thought excitedly. *Maybe I can get first when we go back in the ring. We're definitely a team!*

I was thinking of the ways I could improve my performance when I heard the motor home engine roar to life. Doreen was at the wheel as the huge vehicle trundled out of the fairgrounds and down the road, leaving me with nothing but a snoot full of dust. They hadn't even offered me breakfast.

"Eleventh place in the *finals* wasn't good enough for you?" I howled at them. "I won two ribbons in this show!"

I tore off my newest prize with my teeth and left it at the abandoned campsite. So much for being adored. I'll bet my second-place award never sees the light of day, having been permanently forgotten in Dwayne's coat pocket.

Back Again

Most dogs would say it's crazy to run *to* a shelter, but it was close, and by now the fairgrounds were emptying. I knew The BARC would feed me and give me a blanket to sleep on. They'd done that many times. It was only a couple of miles away, so I jogged down the side of the highway until the familiar building came into view.

I'm in and out of here so often, I thought sourly, *why not just install a revolving door? It would save everyone the effort of having to get up and open it.*

I scratched at the front entry until one of the volunteers answered.

"Poor guy!" she said, not recognizing me at first. "Are you a leftover from the PoodlePalooza?"

Yep. That's exactly what I was. A leftover. But not just any leftover. I was the number one, all-time, world's biggest loser leftover. I gave her my best puppy eyes and she let me in.

Not surprisingly, kennel 2-B was empty. My smells were still there. And now I was back too.

A voice from next door said, "My nose tells me 2B has returned, but my eyes tell me differently."

"Hey, Maurice," I answered. "It's me."

"And all smartened up, I must say," he said. "What was the occasion?"

"A dog show," I responded wearily from under my stiffly sprayed pompadour.

And then I lay down and fell into a deep but fitful sleep.

I awoke in the early evening to find Maurice staring at me.

"Care to share over a bowl of the dry stuff?" he asked.

"Sure," I agreed, knowing how Maurice liked eating together. The kennel attendant with the gentle soapy smell brought our food and, like before, we pushed the two bowls next to our common wire wall.

"I tried my hardest but, I have to say, dog shows are not my cup of kibble," I said between mouthfuls.

"Tell me all about it," Maurice said. He listened quietly as I filled him in on the adventure. I finished up with the final competition where I'd come in eleventh.

"The Show, Glow, and Go lifestyle is a real tail drooper," I concluded. "It's full of nervous, hypercompetitive cutthroats who look like a million barks on the outside. That's not me."

"So," said Maurice thoughtfully, "who is the real you?"

"It's here underneath all these layers of perm, dye, gel, and hair spray," I said.

"Go on," encouraged Maurice.

"I'm just an ordinary dog," I answered. "And like any dog, I want to find my place in this world. But I feel like a piece in one of those jigsaw puzzles. Sadly, my piece won't fit into the picture shown on the box, even when you try pounding it in with a hammer. Maybe I'm from an entirely different puzzle."

"Phillipe used to enjoy putting those together," Maurice observed. "I don't ever remember him using a hammer to make a piece fit, though."

"It's just a saying," I answered wearily.

I flopped back down on the concrete, discouraged. I had given one hundred and ten percent to my last adoption and I had failed, just like every other time.

"So much for the Furry DogMother idea, Maurice. I made a wish like you suggested."

"It was not meant to be, 2B."

"Maybe I'm not adoptable. Maybe The BARC is it for me," I said sadly.

"I think not," Maurice replied. "There is a special place for every dog in this world. Of this, I am quite sure."

I wished I shared Maurice's confidence. But then, he had been in a loving home since he was a tiny pup. What did he know about a life of rejection?

"Your fortunes will rise like a well-baked soufflé," Maurice assured me.

But I had seen plenty of Dragana's soufflés rise, only to collapse when they were taken out of the oven.

Teammates

Two days later a big, burly man burst into The BARC. "How are y'all?" he inquired at the front desk. "Got any loaner dogs here? I'm in serious need of a hunter. My hound came down with a rumble in his gut early this mornin'."

"We do have a couple of residents that might fit the bill," the clerk answered. "Let me show you."

They walked a short way down the hall to where Maurice was housed.

"This is a purebred basset hound. Bassets, as you may know," said the clerk, "are trained to track foxes and badgers."

Maurice rose slowly and moved to the front of the enclosure, his long ears dragging on the cement floor.

"I'm lookin' for a bird dog," the man said. "Besides, this guy don't got much pep in his step. What else you got?"

"Next door, in 2-B, we have a resident who's a bird dog. He's long-legged and eager."

They were standing in front of my kennel run now.

"That's a froufrou poodle dog," the man protested.

"Poodles were originally bred to retrieve ducks," the clerk responded.

"Well," said the man, scratching his beard, "I'll take 'em both. Two loaner noses'll be better'n nothin'."

Maurice and I were about to become a team.

As we bumped along back roads in the bed of a pickup truck, I asked him, "What kind of gig do you think this is?"

"Gig?" asked Maurice.

"Yeah. You know, this temporary job," I answered.

"The gentleman who has borrowed us indicated we would be hunting some sort of flighted game. I, for one, am delighted to explore beyond the confines of The BARC," Maurice answered.

"Yeah," I answered. "Me too. It's great to get out of that place."

"It is a comfortable hostel," Maurice remarked. "The food could be better, but the volunteers are quite nice."

"It's not a real home," I observed.

"That is true," Maurice admitted. "But 2B, you will find your place."

My place. Where was it? My new friend's comment reminded me of the saddest day of my life. It was the day Dragana had come home from Culinary Academy, waving a paper at me.

"Look, Wonder Nose. My diploma. I've graduated! And I was top of my class, with invitations to work at gourmet restaurants in Rome, Hong Kong, Paris, London, and Dubai! Next week I leave for a new job. I'll be cooking in an amazing restaurant . . . but . . . I can't take you with me."

I was in shock. My heart splintered into more pieces than a sheet of Dragana's delicious cracked peanut brittle. I sat and licked her fingers just as I had done the first time we had met. What more could I do? Tearfully she hugged me and said, "You'll find another good home."

I could only hope.

Snuffles and Truffles

The truck slowed and pulled to a stop in the middle of a grassy, wooded area. Other trucks with dogs were already there. Our driver hopped out of the cab and hurried over to them.

"Sorry to be late, gents," he said. "Had to make a detour and pick up a couple of extra hounds."

"Why, Vern, don't tell me that's a poodle in your truck!" guffawed one man.

"It's a perfectly legit hunter," answered our driver defensively. "They're bird dogs."

"He looks like a fancy-pantsy show dog," the man said.

Our driver ignored the comments about me and came striding back to the truck.

"All right, boys. Let's go get 'em." He unlocked the tailgate and lifted out Maurice. I jumped down by myself. We both gave nose to tail body shakes, glad to be out where we could follow our sniffers. This was going to be fun!

Vern pulled some ripe bird wings out of his pack and gave us a big whiff. So this was what we were looking for! The breeze was light, perfect for me to pick up those smells in the wind.

Maurice, on the other paw, had his nose near the ground. We looked at each other.

"Sniff Safari!" I howled.

"Sniff Safari, indeed!" Maurice bayed.

And we took off as only free, happy dogs can. We ran far and wide, taking in the sights, sounds, and, of course, the smells of the area. We tumbled through creeks, raced across grassy meadows, stuck our snouts into bushes, and chased squirrels and birds.

Gradually I could feel the dog show peeling away from me. The perm and dye would wear off over time, I knew from listening to Doreen and her customers. And my coat would grow back in as well. The gels, hair sprays, conditioners, and shampoos were disappearing quickly. I was starting to feel less like a Dandy Dog and more like myself.

"This really is the dog's life!" I barked to Maurice.

"And there is life in *this* old dog yet!" he exulted, trundling farther afield.

As we continued our hunt, I noticed Maurice's ears dragging on the ground.

"Do they bother you?" I asked him. "Your ears?"

"They are referred to as *leathers*," he answered. "And au contraire, they are a huge help to me. They are intended to be like large scoops, ladling smells to my nose as a chef ladles soup into a bowl."

"Hot diggety dog!" I exclaimed. "That is way cool. I wish my ears did that."

"We bassets are designed as we are for good reason. We are close to the ground with large ears and wide necks so we can capture scents near and under the dirt. You, 2B, are designed to gather smells from the air. With your lanky legs, shorter ears, and long, slender snout, you are made to scent through tall grass and bushes. Where you go high, I go low. Together we lock onto every whiff and odor. In this way, we are an excellent pair."

We were in a grove of pecan trees and he started digging with those sturdy legs of his.

"Ahrooo-la-la! I smell truffles," he bayed.

Suddenly I remembered Dragana cooking with truffles. They are ugly misshapen fungi, but their aroma is out of this world. I was familiar with that rich, earthy smell. They are difficult to find and expensive. But on a few occasions, Dragana had splurged and used some in her recipes. She always found the best ingredients. She was a human wonder, cooking up edible wonders.

Maurice was definitely right. He had found truffles. I began to dig too.

TWEEEET! Vern's whistle was calling us in.

We each grabbed one of those gnarly lumps in our mouths and ran back to the truck.

We set them at his feet.

"What in tarnation are these things?" he asked us grumpily. "Sure don't look nothin' like birds to me, boys."

"Vern!" said one of the other hunters. "Don't you realize what those are? Those're them fancy-eatin' truffles. They're worth their weight in hound dogs."

"What do I do with 'em?" Vern asked his friend.

"Why, you sell 'em to one of them highfalutin restaurants. Chefs go crazy over those ugly dug-ups."

"Think there're any more of 'em out there?" Vern asked.

"Wouldn't hurt to camp out for a few days and see," his friend answered.

So our one-day hunt became a several-day adventure. We would get up in the mornings and let our noses do the work. We found enough truffles to fill a cardboard box Vern had in the back of his pickup.

Back to The BARC

Almost a week later we were back at The BARC, worn out from all that truffle hunting. We didn't find many birds, but Vern didn't seem to mind. I think selling the truffles made him think he had been barking up the wrong tree, if you know what I mean.

"That was the best time I have had since Phillipe died," Maurice told me.

"It was fun for me too," I said. "You know, Maurice, I've been wondering. Do you think a nose is a dog's best friend?"

"I do, 2B. With a superior sniffer, the whole world is one's oyster. We can do anything, go anywhere with these noses."

We were feeling cocky after our days out in the fields and our discovery of those truffles. What dog wouldn't? Especially shelter dogs like us. We didn't get out much. Well, I seemed to get out quite a bit—but I also seemed to come back quite a bit.

The BARC put Maurice back into kennel 3-B with me next door in my usual 2-B run. As I waited for prospective owners to visit the shelter and Maurice waited for Perline, the days turned into weeks, and the weeks into a few months. My coat grew back, and the perm and dye faded. We shared meals and memories. Maurice, I discovered, was quite the storyteller.

"Ahh! I remember the time I took an entire ball of Mimolette from the cheese shop next to our restaurant in Paris," he said late one afternoon near to feeding time. "Quietly putting my paws on the counter, I managed to snag it while the customer was examining some foie gras. I must have looked like I had a large cantaloupe wedged in my mouth. Slinking out the front door, I glanced left and then right to see if anyone was on the sidewalk outside . . ."

Demonstrating, Maurice moved his head, and his ears swung heavily from side to side.

"The coast was clear. So out I trotted, cool and smooth as a bowl of vichyssoise."

"What's that?" I interrupted.

"It is a delicious French soup that is eaten cold," he answered. Then he continued on with his tale. "I hurried around the corner and started to eat that stolen cheese. Before I could finish, the woman who had purchased it discovered me. She brandished her shopping bag quite fiercely. I had no choice but to abandon the uneaten part and escape down a side street. I have always regretted leaving so fine a cheese on a city sidewalk. It had such a sweet, nutty flavor."

Maurice started to drool at the memory.

It was then that the kennel keeper arrived with our kibble. He noticed Maurice's drippy lips and said, "Hungry, old boy? Here you go."

He opened our runs to give us our food when . . .

KABOOM! BOOM! BOOM!

A massive explosion rocked The BARC. Concrete chunks rained down around us. Soaked in cold, stale-smelling fire sprinkler water, we scrambled around, crashing into other dogs loose in the shelter. Sirens were wailing in the distance while our kennel mates were howling all around us.

"Go, go, go!" yelled our shelter keepers, grabbing mutts by the collars and pulling them out of the mess.

"Come on, Maurice!" I barked. "Let's hit the road. *Now!*"

With smoke billowing everywhere in burnt-smelling black clouds, we raced on shaky legs out the front door with the crowd and then, scared and overwhelmed, we kept on going down the highway, toward a rest stop.

There were plenty of cars and people milling about there, sidelined from further travel on the roads. Everyone was talking about the unexpected blast.

A crowd had gathered around a television reporter who was broadcasting information on what had taken place.

"A short time ago, an explosion ripped through The BARC dog shelter, destroying much of the structure. Emergency personnel are on the scene. All animals and their caregivers appear to have escaped unharmed. Firefighters are working to contain the blaze. The cause of the incident is currently unknown. Investigators have been called in to examine the site. Further details will be forthcoming. This is Hannah Maxwell with BIG TV, live from Rest Area 11 on State Highway 27."

Maurice and I were at a loss for barks. Nothing could describe the catastrophe and the destruction of our home, The BARC. Where did that leave us?

It left us, first of all, hungry. Supper was on the table, so to speak, when we had been interrupted by the blast.

"Would it be inappropriate, in such a tragic moment, to think about eating?" Maurice asked me.

"It's probably the best thing we can do," I answered. "Full stomachs will allow us to concentrate on what to do next."

We became a couple of serious chow hounds, digging through the trash cans that were placed around the rest area. What we found was truly a dog's dinner with a bit of everything you could imagine. Sort of like a potluck minus the luck.

"*Wurff, wurff!*" snuffled Maurice. "I have found a savory sausage!"

"That's technically a hot dog," I informed him. "Nothing to get too excited about."

"A sausage by any other name is still a sausage," he responded. He wolfed it down while I busied myself with part of a very ripe egg salad sandwich. We ate until we were stuffed. Drinks for the evening came from the toilets. You do what you have to.

"After such a repast," Maurice said, "I feel ready for a nap."

I had to agree. It was quite dark now. The fire was out, and people were leaving the rest stop.

"Let's tour the grounds," I suggested, "to see if we can find somewhere to crash for the night. I'm dog-tired."

We trotted around a building and decided to settle down under a picnic table away from the parking lot. We curled up side by side to preserve our warmth. It was a two-dog night, cold but not freezing.

Maurice fell asleep quickly and started to snore. I, too, fell into a deep slumber but was awakened by a stinky-egg odor that made me want to gag.

"Double Dog Drafts, Maurice!"

"Huh? What?" he stammered.

"The stink!" I choked.

"Excusez-moi. We bassets have delicate stomachs, and digestion is further complicated by substandard foods such as our recent dinner."

"No apologies needed. Just go pass your basset gas someplace else," I told him. I'd rather sleep cold than have to smell that stench.

Maurice grunted and hefted himself up, moving under a nearby picnic table.

The rest of the night passed in cool but sweet-smelling silence.

A New Day

There's a saying that curiosity kills cats. As dogs, we have no such worries.

So early the next morning I said to Maurice, "Let's head back and check out The BARC."

Twisted metal and broken concrete slabs surrounded us when we arrived at our former home.

"Very little of our shelter remains," observed Maurice.

"It was a pretty big boom," I answered. I lifted my nose and smelled something vaguely familiar. Then it dawned on me. I recognized this distinctive odor from a couple of occasions at Dragana's apartment as she cooked late into the evenings.

"Natural gas!" I exclaimed. "This smells exactly like a stove that's been turned on when the flame doesn't light. If you strike a match, place it by the burner, then . . . *fwoof* . . . up comes the fire."

Maurice had his nose down, snuffling and snorting. "You are correct, 2B," he announced. "Do you see these mango-size chunks of metal? They are remains of a gas pipe. I would wager it was part of the basement heating system for The BARC. So yes, it was like a stove, but much bigger. More gas, a bigger pipe, some small spark, and a huge *FWOOF*."

"The *FWOOF* was the explosion," I added.

Brumble brumble brumble.

A van was pulling up where the front of The BARC had been. Behind it was a police car. Maurice and I made ourselves scarce, hiding behind a pile of rubble.

Both drivers got out of their vehicles.

"Good morning, officer. I'm Ginger Georges, owner and operator of Working Like a Dog, the accident investigation company."

A young wiry woman, Ginger seemed to me to be perfectly named. She smelled faintly like a warm welcoming kitchen after a day of baking pies: cinnamon, nutmeg, a hint of lemon, and, of course, ginger.

"Mornin', Ms. Georges. Thanks for meeting me here. I'm Officer Stanley Mieczyslaw, detective for Jacksonville

Police. Let me know how you wish to proceed and how I can help."

"Thank you, Officer Mie . . ah . . . Mia . . ." Ginger said.

"Just call me Officer M. The last name's a mouthful," he said, smiling broadly.

"I'll be bringing my dog Riot out to sniff through the area," Ginger explained. "I've specially trained her to search and locate explosion origins."

"Amazing what these dogs can do," he answered.

"You're doggone right!" I whispered to Maurice. We could hear everything, but our line of vision was partly blocked by the van.

"We've certainly got to respect their noses," Ginger said to Officer M. "They can smell about a hundred thousand times better than humans, so Riot will determine where the blast came from and what caused it. Their noses are their best assets."

"It was natural gas from the old iron pipes in the basement furnace," said Maurice. "We already figured that out."

We could see Ginger bring Riot out of the van, leaving the back doors wide open. This dog was so focused on her job that she ignored our scents and went straight to work. Ginger and Officer M followed her.

"That Riot has concentration," Maurice said admiringly.

"Which means we can make our move," I answered.

"And that is?" he asked.

"Right into the back of that van. Look, Maurice. We don't have a dog shelter anymore. You heard what this Ginger lady does. She trains dogs to use their noses and find things. We passed test number one by already figuring out what happened to The BARC. And we found truffles out in the middle of nowhere. This might be what we're waiting for. After all, we've got the noses that know."

Up and In

"**R**eady? One, two, and up!" I cheered. I was already in the back of the van, which was filled with dog leads, backpacks, safety vests, ropes, GPS devices, shovels, and crates, and I was trying to encourage Maurice. He hadn't been able to bound up high enough to get in.

It was an easy three-foot jump. I had made it well over a dozen times, demonstrating to Maurice the finer points of leaping into a vehicle.

"Get a running start," I advised him.

Maurice came sprinting toward the van. With Maurice, *sprinting* was a relative term. It was more like a quick, clumsy waddle-walk.

Clunk.

Maurice slammed into the bumper.

"Ouch!" he whimpered, picking himself up and shaking off some dust.

"Maybe back up a bit more," I counseled, "and put some spring into your legs."

Maurice looked down at his stubby limbs. "They are not really designed to be springable," he said sadly.

"Just visualize a flying liftoff. Put those big, floppy ears into play. They could act as wings."

Maurice took my advice, ran toward the open back of the van, tried to lift his ears, and leaped.

"Plane crash," he said dejectedly, after he bounced off the bumper once again. He sat down.

"Phew," he puffed. "What a workout! I have not been this tired since I toured the Louvre."

"What's the Louvre?" I asked.

"It is a world-famous French art museum."

"You were allowed inside a museum?" I could hardly believe this.

"Once," Maurice said. "They held a fundraiser for endangered animals there, so pets were admitted with their owners. I remember an iguana on a leash, a potbellied pig in a stroller, and a de-scented skunk. Phillipe and I walked and walked, looking at all sorts of famous paintings. I had sore dogs for weeks."

"You've lived a colorful life, Maurice. But back to business. How do we get you into this vehicle?"

Maurice said, "What if I put my front paws on the bumper like it is a kitchen counter? Then I can ease my back legs up and roll into the van."

"Now you're barking!" I cheered.

Maurice had both front paws firmly planted on the bumper with one back leg just about there when the other leg slipped and he fell back again.

"It is no use, 2B," he whimpered.

"Friend-to-friend advice here, Maurice. No whining!" I jumped out of the van and said, "I'm going to push you from behind. Get those front paws up there again!"

Maurice was almost inside when we heard footsteps coming our way. I gave him one final shove, jumped in myself, and squeezed into a corner under some tarps. Riot hopped into the front passenger seat with Ginger at the wheel. Officer M slammed the back van doors shut, slid into his police car, and drove away. The van slowly wound its way around the yellow caution tape that festooned what had once been The BARC's driveway and headed out for the open road.

"Close call, eh, Maurice?" I said. "But we made it."

When Maurice didn't answer, I stuck my head out from under the tarp. He was nowhere I could see or, more importantly, smell. I glanced out the back window and saw him sitting forlornly off to the side of the drive-way, watching us disappear.

Au Revoir, Maurice

I had been on my own plenty during my life. Being by myself was something that usually didn't bother me.

"Well, Maurice," I said to the empty air, "you'll figure something out. It was nice knowing you." But I was kidding myself. Maurice was the first friend I had made in a long time. I wished my new buddy was by my side, sharing this adventure.

As sad as I was feeling, the van ride was soothing after such a tumultuous two days, and I fell into a deep sleep.

"*Heh-heh-heh.*"

"What have we here?"

The panting and question woke me with a start. The van had stopped. Opening an eye, I could see Riot and Ginger staring at me.

"A stowaway?" asked Ginger.

I stood up, stretched, and walked over to my new lifeline.

Ginger gently put out her hand, and I gave it a half-hearted lick. She stroked me behind my ear and slid her fingers around to my dog tag.

"*2B The BARC*," she read.

"Makes sense. You must have jumped in while we were investigating the explosion site. Nothing left there for you, 2B. The least we can do is take you back to our place to figure out your next steps. But first, I've got to run into the pet store for some kibble."

After rolling down the windows partway to give me some fresh air, she and Riot closed the door and were off. I watched them out the back window. As I did, a large delivery van pulled in across the parking lot, and the driver got out. He, too, went into the pet food store.

I continued gazing out the window, the same window where I had last seen Maurice sitting alone as we had driven away from the ruins of The BARC. My throat felt tight and my heart ached.

Maurice, I thought. *We had some fun times together. I'm gonna miss you.*

Then I did a little jump start and bumped my nose on the glass. At that very moment, I could see a dog that looked suspiciously like Maurice sitting up high in the passenger seat of that delivery van.

A while later, the driver came bounding out of the pet store with a small bag of what appeared to be dry dog food. He threw it onto the seat with the dog that looked like Maurice, and off they drove.

Actually, that wasn't a dog that looked like Maurice. I would have bet my nose it was the real Maurice. How did I know? When the driver opened the door to climb in, a certain scent wafted out. The scent known as basset gas. The man had the windows rolled down as he navigated out of the parking lot and back onto the road.

Moments after Maurice's departure, Ginger and Riot returned with some sizable bags of kibble. Ginger hefted them into the back, and off we went.

I stared through the front windshield of the van. I could make out the delivery truck ahead of us, Maurice's snout out the window, his leathers flapping in the breeze.

Follow that delivery truck! I wished. But Maurice's Furry DogMother was either asleep or on vacation, and the truck vanished into the distance. Riot was snoring after her hard morning's worth of sniff detection, and Ginger was concentrating on driving.

I had lost my only two real friends in this life: First Dragana and now Maurice.

New Headquarters

"**O**K, 2B. Hop out, pup," Ginger said.

We had pulled up to a small farmhouse out in the country. Next to it was a dog kennel that could house a handful of dogs, five to be exact. It reminded me of The BARC but much smaller. It looked clean and well-kept.

"Riot," said Ginger. "Let's show 2B his temporary digs."

After a very quick tour of my run, I ate a bowl of kibble and drank deeply from my water bucket. Satisfied, I turned around a few times on the blanket Ginger had given me and prepared to go to sleep.

"So, what's your tale?" I heard from the next-door run. Since Riot and I were the only dogs there, I knew it had to be her. Still, I was surprised as she hadn't said anything to me until then.

"A bushy tail, just a stray dog with a bushy tail . . . and an exploded former home," I answered.

She was a serious one, that Riot. She didn't even crack a dog smile over my word play with *tail* and *tale*.

"I was a stray once too," she answered. "Actually I was a stray for most of my life, in and out of homes and in and out of shelters. I never seemed to fit in anywhere until I came here."

My ears perked up, and my sleepiness left me. "Really? Why was that?"

"I'm a working dog," she answered. "I was born to work, and that's what we do here."

I was intrigued. "What exactly do you do?"

"I'm a sniff detective," she announced proudly. "Certified and licensed."

"Might be right up my alley," I said.

"We're looking for a couple of good dogs. We have Agnes and Irene, but they're away in Tanzania scouting out elephant scat."

"Sounds exotic," I replied, wondering where Tanzania was and what elephant scat was.

"Yeah," said Riot. "But it's a long trip in a dog crate halfway around the world in the belly of an airplane, so there are some downsides to the job."

"Do you travel much?" I asked her.

"No, I usually do domestic assignments. Things like explosions, accidents, and smuggling. I work with police, fire, airports, city departments, stuff like that," she explained.

"Is it dangerous?" I asked.

"It can be, but I'm very well trained so I'm not concerned." She yawned and circled around on her blanket, signaling that she was done talking and ready to sleep.

"So, how do I get a job here?" I asked her as her eyes were shutting down for the night.

"Demonstrate what your nose knows," she muttered sleepily, and then all I could hear was her deep and rhythmic breathing.

Job Interview

My nose knows a lot, I thought when I woke up the next morning. How could I show Riot and, more importantly, Ginger I had a sniffer worth hiring?

Riot's information the night before had focused and energized me. Maybe I had finally arrived at the place I was meant to be.

Ginger fed us and let us out to roam the property. Sniff Safari all over again. It reminded me of Maurice, and I hoped he was OK, wherever he was.

Out in the back field there were three white boxes standing tall.

"What are these?" I asked Riot.

"Beehives," she answered. "Ginger harvests her own honey."

There was a wild melody of smells around those hives. I could detect the sweetness of several types of flowers.

Riot told me, "The bees gather pollen and bring it to the hives to make the honey. Right now they're all bundled up inside, settling down for the winter. But you have to be careful during the spring and summer. They're out in force then, and they won't hesitate to sting you on the nose if you get in their flight path."

An injured nose was the last thing I needed. Who knew honey could be so dangerous? Dragana had used it when she baked, and in her tea in the mornings. I thought it came from a jar.

Ginger walked out toward the hives carrying some pliers and wire. I could see her crouching down and bending over, crouching down and bending over, weaving the wire through some holes in a fence. After a while, she straightened up and called us in. Gray skies told me it might snow, so instead of being returned to our kennels, we were actually invited inside the house.

Ginger was sitting at her computer logging on when she said, "Now where did I put my phone? Everything from The BARC explosion is on it . . . pictures, videos, and voice notes. I need to file my report and bill the police department for our work. I was looking through it all during breakfast."

She rummaged through stuff on her desk and came up empty. "Did I leave it on the kitchen table?" she wondered aloud. But only her empty tea mug and a sticky half-full jar of honey were there.

Ginger continued to look but found nothing.

"Doggone it!" she exclaimed. "I need to find my phone!"

She spent time rifling through much of her small house, but she still came up empty-handed.

I watched her and thought. She had her phone at The BARC and at breakfast. *Hmmm.*

I scratched to go out. Ginger got up and opened the door for me.

Once outside, I lifted my nose in the cold, still morning air. What was I hunting for? Traces of honey and natural gas aromas mixed together was my guess. Now that's got to be a unique combination. Honey from Ginger's breakfast and natural gas from The BARC explosion. I never forget scents once they're stored in my brain. Both of these were very recent and fresh in my head, and I couldn't smell them together in the house.

I concentrated and waited. After a while, I could vaguely make out both scents mingled together. I followed my nose, which is easy since it's far out on the front of my face. I trotted toward those beehives. But snowflakes gently floating down complicated the scent direction. Which way was it coming from?

"2B, come!" Ginger had poked her head out of the door. "Come!" she called again.

But I couldn't obey her quite yet. I was getting close to the smells I thought would lead me to her phone.

Obedience was very important to her. I could tell because she said, "If you don't come now, I guess you'll stay out here on your own."

Then she disappeared back inside.

Still, I had to risk it. This was my job interview. I ignored her commands and hoped she would understand. I trotted off, zigzagging through the field, left and right and left and right. Nothing, yet the smell was still there somewhere. It seemed low down. I wished Maurice were here to help. His nose was so good with smells near the ground.

Come on, 2B, I told myself. *A nose is a dog's best friend. Don't let me down now, Wonder Nose!*

Eventually, my friend Wonder Nose led me to that fence Ginger had repaired. I trotted along it. Halfway down, partly covered with a dusting of snow, was the phone. I took it carefully in my mouth and hurried back to the house. It was snowing more heavily now.

I scratched to be let in, but there was no answer.

What now? I wondered. It was getting colder and more snow was falling. I scratched again but no answer. I couldn't just stand here. Either I had to get in or I would stay outside and freeze into a pupsicle.

Riot came to my rescue, dear girl that she is.

"*Roofff, roofff, roofff!*" She had a deep, commanding bark. She stopped barking only when Ginger opened the door. There I stood with the missing phone cradled in my mouth.

"2B!" she said. "Didn't I already. . . . Wait! What's that?"

I gently dropped it at her feet, hoping it wouldn't break. I watched her.

"Ohhh!" she gasped. "My phone! 2B, you found this outside? It must have slipped out of my pocket when I was mending the fence." She pulled me in, snow slop and all, and gave me a big hug.

"You've got a special nose. It's just the kind I could use. Looking for a job, big guy?"

This was the news I had wanted to hear. I gave her big slurpy dog kisses all over her delicately scented face while my tail thumped uncontrollably.

I think I just got hired!

An Unexpected Visitor

The next few weeks were sleety. It was too wet and cold to be out training, so Riot and I continued to enjoy Ginger's home hospitality during the day, especially her fireplace. It had such a toasty, snuggly aroma. We were both plopped down on a rug near the hearth. I was falling into a dog dream about Dragana and a very meaty soup bone when there was a light rap on the door.

Ginger got up from her computer and answered it.

"How may I help you?" she asked politely.

"Excusez-moi," said a slight, older woman with a French accent. "My name is Perline Babineux, and I am searching for information on the explosion at a dog shelter called The BARC."

"Come in," said Ginger. "My dog Riot and I determined the cause of that blast."

"Yes." Perline nodded eagerly. She stamped slush from her boots and came through the door. "The police kindly gave me your address. I am wondering if you know what happened to the animals from the shelter. My late brother's dog was temporarily housed there until I could fly over from France to retrieve him. A basset hound."

I was all ears now. This had to be Phillipe's sister, come to get Maurice and take him back to Paris!

"I wish I could help you," Ginger said. "When I arrived on scene, all the dogs had been evacuated. Some ran away. In fact, that dog over there was a shelter stray I picked up on site. But he was all by himself."

Perline looked disappointed, and she smelled genuinely sad: cold, misty, and metallic. "Thank you," she said. "I will leave you my contact information should you discover anything about Maurice. It would mean so much to have him back. That dog is my last connection to my wonderful brother, and I so wish to find him."

She showed Ginger a picture of Maurice and Phillipe on her phone.

"What a sweet twosome!" Ginger said. "I can tell they had a special bond."

"Oh yes," agreed Perline. "They were inseparable."

"With your permission, I'll scan this picture and send it out to other local pet shelters," Ginger suggested.

Perline smiled. "But of course!"

Before she left, she came over and gave me a gentle pat on the head. "Perhaps you knew Maurice, my sweet furry friend. We loved him so much."

Then she thanked Ginger and left. My heart was breaking for Maurice, wherever he was.

Learning the Ropes

"Time to learn the ropes, 2B," Ginger said to me one morning in early spring.

I had heard those words before when I lived on a sailboat with a lady named Bambi. There were lots of ropes connected to the sails that made that boat fly through the water. Bambi was always pulling on them or coiling them. I wasn't sure how ropes were part of my life now, but I was eager to find out. As it turned out, ropes in this case were actual smells. Yes, I had to learn many, many new smells.

The winter had passed, and it was time to get serious about Sniff School training.

On my first day, we started off with a long walk around the farm. This was a free roam, and Riot came along. We sniffed everywhere.

Maurice would love this, I thought, remembering our hunting trip. *I miss my old buddy.*

While we rambled, Ginger pulled a tube of hair gel from her pocket and began squirting globs of it out in the field near our kennels. Hair gel, in my opinion, was a strange way to train a dog to be a sniff detective, but I was just a know-nothing novice at that point.

"2B, come," she commanded, letting me sniff the tube. "Go find."

Hair gel was something I thought I would never have to smell again, not after the PoodlePalooza. I'd had more than a snootful of that during my time as a show dog. Still, I obeyed and easily found all nine globs she had squirted in the grass.

"Good dog!" she exclaimed, tossing me a treat.

Over and over, we practiced with the gel. Sometimes she would give commands such as "Go right!" or "Go left!" She pointed, and I went where her fingers showed me. Pretty soon I automatically knew those directions.

The next training step was inside her barn. She had a long wooden plank set on top of some wooden boxes.

There were bowls set on the plank with different items in them.

"2B," Ginger said, waving a stubby stick in front of my nose. "This is cinnamon. Can you find it in a bowl?"

You bet! I thought. But something else was highjacking my nostrils.

Bubblegum.

Pahffff! Pahffff! I blew that strong sweet scent out of my nose slits. Awhile back, I had once chewed up an entire roll of the stuff. It was the reason I had been returned to The BARC after one of my many adoption failures. I was not about to let bubblegum make me a failure again.

Focus, I told myself. *Don't get distracted.*

I walked up and down the plank table, sniffing each container. *Pahffff, pahffff.* I blew out more air. *Wiff.* Then I delicately breathed in through my nostrils.

Ahh! There it was. The spicy, woody smell of cinnamon. Of course, it reminded me of Dragana's breakfast buns, the best ever in my humble opinion.

"*Rowrff! Rowrff!*" I barked. Then I sat directly in front of the container that I thought had the spice.

"Good boy!" complimented Ginger, throwing me one of her tasty dog biscuits.

We practiced for weeks and weeks, and my snout sucked up many smells. I worked on animal scents such as snakes, leopards, and gorillas. I learned about birds, perfumes, and jewelry.

We spent time on wines and cheeses. Maurice would have heartily approved. I whiffed in dirty diapers, which actually smelled a lot like some of those cheeses. I breathed in toothpastes, seeds, and sweaty baseball gloves. I inhaled aromas for fish, fruits, and feathers. Diesel fuel, bug spray, nuts, and flowers. You name it, I sniffed it. And, of course, everything got delivered to my scent memory, not to be forgotten.

Finally, the day came when Ginger said, "Congratulations, 2B! You are a certified Sniff Detective."

She removed my old nylon collar with its BARC dog tag, and around my neck she placed a slim, leather collar with a new tag. Ginger told me it said *2B* on one side and on the other *WLAD,* which stood for our company, Working Like a Dog.

I say *our* company because I was now a full-fledged member of the team. I had worked like a dog and was certified to prove it. It was a proud day for me.

SIT Dog

"Time to go to work, 2B," Ginger said to me early one morning not long after I had graduated.

"Riot, are you coming too?" I asked her.

"That's *Ms.* Riot to you and, yes, I'm coming," she answered.

Riot sounded different, more severe and formal. But I didn't know why.

"Sorry, *Ms.* Riot," I apologized. "Show dogs and queens carry titles. I didn't know you were either."

She cracked a tiny dog smile. "It's really M-S as in Master Sniffer," she said. "You, 2B, are a SIT dog."

Immediately I sat. Having heard that command so often in my training, I'm sure I would do it in my sleep if Ginger ordered it. The mental image of a sound-asleep me suddenly bolting upright slumbery, slobbery, and snoring made me chuckle.

"No, 2B," Riot explained. "A S-I-T dog means Sniffer-in-Training. Today we do real work with real consequences, so put on your serious suit."

My serious suit turned out to be a royal blue vest with a *WLAD Security Dog* patch on it. That made me official. I felt important and also a little nervous.

Riot looked me over with a cool, practiced eye. "You're in uniform now, 2B. Stay calm and professional."

Then we both sprang into the back of the van and we were on our way to . . . I wasn't sure where.

It turned out the airport was our destination. I had never been to one before, and I was fascinated by all the noisy activity.

Nneeaooww. Planes came in for landings. *Vrroomm voor.* Planes took off from the runway. *Brub brub brubbbb.* Gas trucks drove about looking for planes to refuel. If ears had noses, they would be overwhelmed by what they smelled at an airport.

"We'll be working a couple of different areas today," Ginger told us as she clipped leashes onto our collars. "We'll start in the arrivals terminal."

We entered through a side door after Ginger slid her pass across the lock. This put us squarely in the baggage staging area. Rows of suitcases were lined up and ready to be loaded onto the baggage claim conveyor belts.

Snuff, snuff, snuff . . . Riot and I walked up and down the rows, sniffing, sniffing, sniffing.

Lots of interesting aromas, I thought. And then . . . *"Rowrff! Rowrff!"* I sat, as I had been trained, next to the suitcase with the offending smell.

"Good pup!" Ginger praised.

An airport official opened it up and inside were five clear plastic baggies full of seawater and fish nestled among T-shirts, underwear, and socks.

"Look at that!" he exclaimed, plucking them out of the suitcase. "Baby trigger fish. You can't bring wildlife into the country without a permit."

Riot and I continued our work.

"Rowrff! Rowrff!"

An old sword.

"Rowrff! Rowrff!"

Fourth of July fireworks.

The dangerous things humans packed in suitcases. Really. What were they thinking? Eventually it was time for a break. We went outside to a grassy area, peed, ate a few treats, and stretched out in the spring sunshine.

Batabatabatabata.

Looking up, I saw something I had never seen before. It was like an airplane but without wings, just a spinning blur on its top. It was dropping straight down toward the runway.

"Helicopter," Riot informed me.

It landed nearby. The blur slowed to a stop, the door opened, and a man jumped out, walking briskly toward a building. A gasoline tanker pulled up to refuel it.

Then something else jumped out or, should I say, lurched out.

Although my eyes could not believe what I saw, my nose never lies. "Maurice?" I yelped, my heart leaping in my chest.

Reunion

I completely lost my professional composure, as well as my level head, and tore across the tarmac toward my old friend. I leaped onto and over a baggage truck, dodged the gasoline tanker with its thick hose, and brushed by an airplane mechanic in my bid to reach Maurice.

"2B! Come!" yelled Ginger.

"2B, get your dog butt over here!" barked Riot.

"Maurice!" I howled, ignoring them. "Maurice!"

We collided into a heap of happy-houndness.

"2B!" bayed Maurice. "Is it really you, or are my two eyes deceiving me?"

"Oh, it's me all right!" I exclaimed.

By this time, Ginger and Riot had reached us.

"OK, mister," Ginger growled, grabbing me by my new leather collar. "You are grounded."

But I growled right back at her. This was my dearest friend, and I wasn't going to let anyone or anything come between us.

Ginger might have been a strict, by-the-book sort of trainer, but she deeply understood the canine mind. She let go of my collar and stepped back to reassess the situation.

"Oh, poor dog!" she exclaimed, looking at Maurice. "You're covered in blood!"

I'd been too happy to see my dear friend to really *see* him. He *was* covered in blood.

"Maurice," I whimpered. "Are you badly hurt?"

"Mainly in my heart, 2B," he answered.

To her credit, Ginger took control of the situation and immediately brought all three of us back to her van. After Riot and I jumped in, she gently lifted in Maurice. She hopped into the driver's seat, turned on the ignition, punched the accelerator, and we rocketed out of the airport. We didn't stop until we got to the veterinary hospital.

Several hours and many stitches later, Maurice was wheeled out on a gurney and gently placed on a blanket in the back of the van. He was groggy from the anesthetic and snored all the way to the farm. For the first time in memory, according to Riot, all of us dogs spent the night inside Ginger's small house.

As soon as Maurice awakened, I told him about Perline's visit.

"Très magnifique!" he exclaimed weakly. "To see her again will do my heart good. But I will leave a part of it with my new friend Sergio. He was so kind to me. He welcomed me into his home and made me feel wanted and loved." Then he fell back asleep.

That made me think. Maybe I had left part of my heart with my prior owners, especially Dragana. How much of my heart was left?

I hardly left Maurice's side. He wasn't up to his usual storytelling, so I was in the dark as to what had happened and where he had been all these months. But I did gather a few facts when Ginger called Perline.

"Ms. Babineux?" Ginger spoke nervously. "I think we've found your dog. Maurice, right? He was wearing a BARC collar with his name on it. He's torn up pretty badly. The vet pulled glass shards out of his hide. He has seventy-two stitches and a bunch of drains I have to tend to. . . . Yes, lots of hot compresses and antibiotics every day. I think he'll pull through."

She paused and listened.

"Yes, yes. Plan to come and get him in a couple of months. By then he should be fully healed up. . . . Where did I find him? We were at the airport, doing scent detection on baggage for arriving flights. But you won't believe this. . . . He came stumbling off a Medical Emergency Evacuation Helicopter. How he got onto it is beyond me."

The Rest of the Story

A couple days after Maurice's dramatic exit from the helicopter, he was able to get up and move about. Since I was grounded from Sniff Duty, we walked together through the large pastures around the farm. Riot and Ginger went off to detect dangerous smells, so we generally had the place to ourselves.

My curiosity was so great, it would have snuffed out all nine lives of every cat in the country. "How *did* you get onto that helicopter, Maurice?" I asked him eagerly as we were out ambling around one sunny morning.

"That is the end of the story, 2B," he answered.

"So start at the beginning, and we'll get there eventually."

"But of course!" Maurice said. "When we were last together, I believe you were giving me a large push in the derriere. I was so close to staying in the back of that van! But I was off balance and came rolling out just before Officer M arrived and closed the door. All I could see was the underside of the vehicle. I lay there very still, terrified I would be crushed, but thankfully Ginger pulled away slowly."

"I saw you on the side of the destroyed driveway as we left," I said.

"I told myself not to panic," Maurice continued. "I remembered a time several years before when I had been left behind in the Paris Metro. Phillipe and I . . ."

"What's the Paris Metro?" I interrupted.

"It is an underground train system that takes passengers around the city quickly," he answered. "Phillipe and I were near the train door, and when it opened I mistakenly jumped off. *Snap!* The door quickly shut behind me and moved out of the station. I could see Phillipe's panicked face looking out the train window as I was left sitting on the platform.

"A kind man took me upstairs to the ticket booth. The attendant opened the door, and I was taken inside. She wisely looked at my collar. Fortunately, my dog tag had

Phillipe's name and phone number on it. He was contacted, and while I waited for him, the attendant shared a flaky croissant with me. It was quite tasty."

"I've really missed you and your stories," I said to Maurice.

Maurice nodded his head. "And I have missed you as well. But I learned that being left behind can also be the beginning of going on."

I was confused. "How so?"

"I was left behind after Phillipe died," he answered, "but then you came along and off I went again on a new adventure. Then, tout à coup, you were gone too."

"I was," I agreed.

"Highway 27 is a busy road," Maurice continued. "I decided to hike to Rest Area 11 to seek human help. Many vehicles came zooming past, in both directions. *Whoosh! Whoosh!* The updrafts buffeted me about, and I felt quite frightened. But before long, a large delivery van pulled over in front of me and the driver got out.

"He said to me, 'Hey, amigo. Are you lost?' His smells were honorable, so I decided to trust him. I got into his van, and off we drove."

Then Maurice got very quiet. I wondered what he was thinking about.

"The last time I saw you, you were riding shotgun in that delivery van, snout in the breeze. You'd just pulled out of a parking lot near a pet store," I said, trying to get him back into his story.

"Ah, yes!" Maurice said, his eyes brightening. "The driver, a kindhearted man named Sergio, thought I should have something better to eat than donut holes."

"Donut holes?" I repeated.

"They were leftovers from his morning coffee stop. At the time, they were quite delicious, but they did tend to give me the . . . ah . . ."

"The basset gas."

He nodded. "My life became a pleasant routine of accompanying Sergio as he delivered packages, then going home to his house each night. We would eat dinner, and Sergio would study his hiking maps. He loved walking in the woods. We took many weekend strolls together. Such an idyllic time."

"But Maurice," I cut in, "how did you get injured?"

"Yes, yes," he said. "I am getting to that part. Sergio and I had pulled out onto the highway after a delivery when a large 18-wheeler came barreling up behind us. As it tried to pass, it ran us off the road and down a steep embankment. Tumbling over and over, our van crashed through the trees, pieces of glass and metal flying everywhere."

"And that's how you got so cut up," I added.

"*Eeooeooe woowoowoo.*" Maurice bayed his best imitation. "I will never forget that siren sound. There were also lights, noise, and lots of humans.

"Poor Sergio," continued Maurice. "The firefighters had to cut him out of the driver's seat. They loaded him onto a stretcher. A medical helicopter landed in the middle of the highway to pick him up.

"'*Maurice! Maurice!*' I could hear him gasp out my name as they wheeled him away. A kind EMT loaded me into the helicopter too, and off we flew."

I shivered, hearing such a gruesome story.

"It got worse while we were in the air. I heard the nurse say, '*He's flatlining! Flatlining!*' They landed on the roof of a hospital, I think, and rushed him in. I was so frightened, I hid behind a large flight bag. No one thought to look for me, anyway. The helicopter took off again and landed at the airport. You know the rest of the story."

"I'm so happy you made it, Maurice," was all I could choke out.

He nodded, but I could see he was very upset. "I guess I will never know what happened to my new friend, Sergio. I had grown quite fond of him."

Buddy Dogs

The bees were out busily gathering pollen to make honey.

Ginger and Riot had been working lots of sniff assignments.

Agnes and Irene were away in Tanzania checking out elephant poop.

Only Maurice and I were idle, still taking our ease each day by strolling through the fields around the farm.

"'Everyone pulls their weight. There's no free freight,' as Sergio used to say," Maurice remarked. "We should do something to earn our keep around here."

"But you're going home to Paris soon," I reminded him. "Why not just chill?"

"Life is so much more rewarding when one is out doing something good for others," he replied.

"That's true," I admitted, stopping to sniff some of the meadow wildflowers. "But how do we . . . *Ouch! Ouch!*" I yelped. "I've been stu-u-u-ng!"

"Bees!" warned Maurice. "Run for it!"

And we did, straight back to the farmhouse.

Fortunately, Ginger was there, and she saw us hightailing it toward her.

"Uh-oh," she said. "2B, you've met up with a bee." She tenderly pulled the stinger out with a pair of tweezers and iced my poor sniffer. "That'll probably swell up some."

Feeling sorry for myself, I plopped down on the living room rug and tried licking the sore spot with my tongue. Maurice trotted over to the water bowl and was getting a drink when Ginger's phone rang.

"Working Like a Dog, Ginger Georges speaking. How may I help you?" she answered. "Companion dogs for new readers at the library?" She eyed the two of us. "Yes, I have two dogs who might work out well for you."

She hung up and looked at me. "Here's a job you can do even with that nose. Since you and Maurice seem to be pretty tight buddies, I'm sending you out as a pair. All you have to do is listen to little kids reading."

To Maurice she said, "Welcome to the WLAD team. You may be a temporary employee but, nevertheless, you now officially work for the company. I'm giving you a collar in recognition of that." Maurice's old BARC collar was removed and, like me, he was given a leather one with a WLAD tag that Ginger would soon have engraved with his name.

And so our new career was born.

The library was an old building with marble floors and wood-paneled walls. Maurice told me it smelled of the sweet inkiness of books. Comfy couches and chairs were everywhere. Would Maurice and I get to sit in them when we listened to children read? I sure hoped so.

"Hello!" We were greeted by a friendly woman at the front desk. She looked from Ginger to Maurice and me and said, "You must be here to listen to our young readers. How wonderful! The children's section is on the second floor. Ask for Libby when you get there. She'll show you to your space."

Up we went in the elevator. As we stepped out into the lobby, we were greeted by a stunning painting that hung on the wall opposite us. It showed two old-fashioned women sitting in a garden reading a book to a little kid. Even we dogs appreciate fine art when we see it, especially Maurice who's had Louvre experience.

As we stopped to gaze at it, Libby, the children's librarian, approached.

"Beautiful painting, isn't it?" she asked us.

"It's breaktaking," answered Ginger. "I'm going to take it home with me," she joked.

"Ha-ha," laughed Libby. "It's called *The Garden Reading* by Mary Cassatt, but it's one of the few things here in the library you can't borrow."

"*The* Mary Cassatt?" Ginger asked her. "The famous Impressionist painter? How can a public library afford such a work of art?"

"It's on loan from a private collection," answered Libby. "It sure sets the tone for peaceful reading with kids. We love having it here. And we love having you and your dogs here too! Follow me and I'll show you where you can set up."

We were led into a cozy nook with couches and beanbag chairs scattered among shelves of books. Children and adults buzzed about happily, searching for interesting stories. They reminded me of the bees in Ginger's hives, minus the stingers.

"Score one for comfort reading!" I said to Maurice as we were invited to sit on special beanbag chairs for dogs. We settled in and waited for our first customers. Children lined up with their books, eager to read with us.

We heard some interesting stories and were both very attentive listeners. Dogs are good at that, actually. I was really enjoying *Go, Dog. Go!* when an ear-piercing, pulsing sound wailed throughout the entire library.

"Fire alarm!" yelled Libby. "Everyone evacuate!"

Holy hounds! I thought. *Here we go again. First The BARC and now the library. How do Maurice and I always get mixed up in emergency situations like this?* Ginger ran to grab us, and we jostled down the stairwell with little kids crying and big adults bellowing directions. I was relieved when we crashed through the exit door and into the fresh air outside. I stuck my nose up, trying to catch the odor of fire, but that doggone bee sting had swollen up my sniffer so I couldn't smell a thing.

"Sniff anything, Maurice?" I asked.

"Nothing connected to a blaze of any sort," he answered.

A short time later, we were given the all clear. Libby found us and escorted us back up to the second floor to get our belongings.

"Wow," she said as we climbed the stairs and entered the children's section. "Sorry your reading time was interrupted. A false alarm has never happened here before." Then she gasped, pointing to the wall. "The painting! It's gone!" Only its empty frame looked down on us like an open mouth screaming for help.

"Oh no!" exclaimed Ginger.

Soon after Libby's discovery, Officer M hurried into the children's section of the library.

"Ms. Georges!" he called. "It's very fortunate to see you here with some of your sniff detectives. They're just what we need."

"Of course, Officer M." Ginger was all business as she listened to him describe what he knew about the robbery.

"2B, Maurice!" she called. "Sniff!"

And so we began our search. Unfortunately, my nose didn't work. It felt stiff and puffy.

"What've you got, Maurice?" I asked him.

"Interesting floor scents near the painting," he responded. "Dare I say it smells a little like forest? A veritable bouquet of tree leaves and bark. Definitely not an odor one would normally find in a library. Plus, I am catching a delicate whiff of Chanel, which is a famous French perfume," he added. "It is very expensive."

"I can't smell at all," I said miserably. "It's that bee sting."

"Well, my nose works fine," Maurice said kindly. "Let me take it from here."

Maurice moved toward the open elevator door. Head down, he snuffled around inside the small compartment. Then he did something that was completely inappropriate in a library.

"*Ahrooo!*" he bayed, just as he had done when we were hunting for truffles. I am willing to bet Maurice was the first and only dog to ever try that in a library and get away with it.

There, in the corner under the elevator's control panel, was a single jewel.

Retraining

"**T**he PoodlePalooza!" I gasped, rushing inside the elevator for a closer sniff.

"Pardon?" asked Maurice.

"Tall Paul wore a collar at that dog show with jewels that smelled like this," I answered.

"Was he here in the library this afternoon?" Maurice asked me.

"Not that I noticed," I answered. "But, like you, I was busy listening to stories."

By this time, the elevator was starting to get crowded. Officer M was there as well as Ginger and a couple of librarians.

"A diamond, perhaps?" he asked, pulling out a clear plastic bag. He put the jewel into it and then sealed it. "Interesting to find it in here. Since no one was allowed in the elevator during the evacuation, I'm thinking the thief may have used it to slip away undetected. The police department will be happy to pay you for your work this afternoon."

Ginger nodded and thanked Officer M. "Let's go, Dognamic Duo," she told us.

In the van on the way home, Ginger's phone rang. She put it on the hands-free speaker. "Hello. This is Ginger Georges with Working Like a Dog. How can I help you?"

"Greetings, Ginger. This is Officer M," said the deep voice. "Once again, thank you for the last-minute use of 2B and Maurice. They did provide some direction for us."

At the mention of our names, we listened in eagerly.

"Once again, you are very welcome," Ginger responded.

"We've contacted the owners of the stolen painting," he went on. "Needless to say, they are very upset with the theft. They are offering a sizable reward for information on the painting or its recovery. I thought I would see whether you and your dogs might be interested in assisting in the search. Any help would be appreciated by the police. Since all of you were at the scene of the crime, this seems sensible to me."

"But how can my sniff detectives be of service?" Ginger asked. "They're trained for detecting explosives and illegal entry of fruits, vegetables, and fish."

"We would be happy to train them to sniff for some very specific smells for this case," Officer M said.

"Of course!" Ginger answered. "I'd like to include my other dog Riot in the training too, if that's OK."

"That's great!" exclaimed Officer M. "Can you meet me down at police headquarters on Friday to get started?"

"We'll be there," she told him, and then she hung up.

Maurice and I looked at each other. Police Detective Dogs?

"Hey," I said to him. "Should I call you Officer Maurice?"

He gave me a big huff out his nose, the equivalent of a dog laugh, and said, "In France, I would be *Inspector* Maurice."

By the end of the week, my bee sting was a distant memory. Maurice, Riot, and I energetically trit-trotted through the halls of a large Police Training Center. We passed by areas where officers were involved in self-defense, target practice, and physical training.

We entered a small room. As we waited patiently, the door opened and Officer M stepped in.

"Thanks for coming," he said. "As you can see, we've put out a number of scents that relate to art such as paint, linseed oil, charcoal, natural bristle brushes, and turpentine."

The training was very similar to what Riot and I had done with Ginger in the barn. We were just adding more scents to our smell memories. For Maurice it was all new, but being a chef's dog with an experienced nose, he caught on quickly. Ginger and Officer M were strictly business. We worked hard learning art smells as well as antiquities like old jewelry and carvings, and by the end of the day, Riot, Maurice, and I were totally sniffed out.

That evening back at the farm, we talked about the session.

"It was like I was back at the Louvre," Maurice observed. "All those smells make up famous paintings. Except they are better blended together and the aromas are older, of course."

"Older?" Riot asked.

"Yes," he said. "Many works of art were done hundreds of years ago, so the fragrances are more subtle. It is like a fine cheese. The smell of a painting can change as it ripens and ages."

"Interesting," I said. "We've come a long way since our first days together at The BARC."

"Life winds over many roads," Maurice added philosophically.

"I wonder where those roads are taking us," I replied.

"Right here," Riot observed practically.

A Day at the Shore

After an intense couple of weeks of art and antiquities sniff school, Ginger came by our kennel.

"Time off, pups!" she told us. "You've been working and studying hard. You've earned a bit of fun."

Ginger was such a great boss. She knew when to work us like dogs and when to let us dogs be dogs. We climbed into the van and took off down the road.

As we neared our destination, three canine noses went into action.

"Salty air smells," I said.

"I am detecting underlying scents of wet, slightly rotted seaweed," Maurice added.

"Is that rocky, chalky odor sand?" Riot asked.

"*The beach!*" we happily howled together.

All three of us waited, quivering with excitement, while Ginger unloaded the van. She pulled out a towel, a sun umbrella, and a basket with both human and dog treats. This was going to be a great day!

She let us off our leashes to run free as we neared the water's edge.

"Glorious!" I barked, streaking after the plovers and seagulls that had congregated near the waves. Maurice was right with me, a long thread of drool ribboning off his jowls. Riot took off after another dog. We ran and ran, dodging in and out of waves. Other mutts along the beach joined in, and our pack energetically romped up and down the shoreline creating a living, moving fabric of joy.

I stopped in utter happiness and started to dig. A huge cloud of sand sprayed through my back legs as the hole in front of me deepened. Maurice started in as well.

Did life get any better than this?

"Ohhh no!" cried out a nearby voice. "My ring! I've lost my wedding ring!" A woman splashed out of the shallows of the water and grabbed a large beach towel. She sobbed into it, "I'll never find it. It was my great-grandmother's diamond!"

"Did someone mention a diamond?" Maurice asked me.

"For something so rare and valuable to humans, diamonds seem to be everywhere," I observed. "We smelled one in the library elevator, some in our police training, and now here at the beach."

We looked at each other and jumped back into duty. Riot, down the beach, was out of reach. We moved toward the lady. As we approached, she removed her floppy beach hat and tried to shoo us away. Ignoring her flimsy weapon, we gave her a sniff-over, along with her towel and her beach bag. We sniffed around her children and their sand toys. From our smell memories we downloaded *diamond* and mixed that with what we had just breathed in.

The search was on. And in this case, two noses were definitely better than one. I stood on the wet sand while Maurice waded into the shallows. I pointed my snout into the breeze.

"Dawgabunga!" howled Maurice.

I turned back to look, and there he was, body surfing the tiny shore waves, his leathers floating out from either side of his large, wrinkly head. I had to smile. This guy lived life to the fullest.

He trotted over to me, shaking the water off himself. "That was a fine ride! No scent of the diamond in the water near the shore that I could detect. Certainly the ring could have been carried out deeper with the waves."

"Maurice, how could any dog smell underwater?"

"It is quite simple, 2B. The gases from certain objects rise through the water and up into the air. There they can be scented. Diamonds give off a delicate carbon gas. The smell is slightly acidic."

"I'm thinking it's a four-in-one smell combo on this one," I informed him. "Perhaps a mix of sunscreen, tuna sandwiches, corn chips, and diamond."

Again, I lifted my nose and concentrated, filtering out distracting odors. I felt like the scents were starting to come together. I trotted over to a sandcastle near the water's edge. The incoming waves were nibbling away at the moat, washing it back into the ocean.

I started to delicately scratch away on the beach side of the structure.

"Mommy!" cried one of the woman's children. "That doggy is wrecking our castle!"

"*Rowrff!*" I barked, sitting immediately as I had been trained to do. There, peeking out of a sand tower, was a large, sparkling diamond ring. I delicately pulled it out and delivered it to the lady.

"I . . . I . . . I can't believe it!" she stuttered through her tears. "It must have slipped off when we were creating our castle. I thought I lost it in the water." She slipped it back onto her finger and grabbed me around the neck, giving me an eyeball-popping hug.

Maurice came trotting over.

"*Howlzer!*" he bellowed happily. "You've got a brilliant nose, 2B! Simply the best!"

Maybe I did, but it was being able to analyze and combine the smells that had led me to the lost ring. Was this a special talent all my own? I wasn't sure.

By this time, Ginger had approached the woman and was telling her about us. "They're specially trained sniff detectives," she said proudly.

"This is am-a-a-a-zing!" squealed the lady. She pulled out her phone. "Can you take a few pictures of me with your dog . . . what's his name?"

"He's called 2B," Ginger said, giving my head a fond ruffle.

So we posed together, her holding up her hand with her ring, and me smiling proudly into the camera lens.

"Do you mind if I post this on my social media?" she asked. "Otherwise, no one will believe this story."

Ginger smiled graciously. "Of course not. By the way, he is employed with my company, Working Like a Dog. Feel free to mention that as well."

Apparently, this lady had a huge internet following because before long, our story went viral. That meant everyone knew about it.

24-Karat Nose

"**L**ook at this!" crowed Ginger one morning a few days after I had found the diamond ring. She held up her phone, and I could see my picture on it. "2B! You're getting famous. Check out the headline. It says '24-Karat Nose Knows Where to Find Carats.'"

I sat next to her, my head cocked, listening.

She looked at me and laughed. "OK. OK. I'll read you the article:

> On a sandy stretch of beach, canine Sniff Detective 2B found the proverbial needle in the haystack.

Only this was no needle but an antique diamond wedding ring weighing two carats owned by Ms. Elizabeth Harold.

'I was playing with my children, both in and out of the water, when I noticed my wedding ring was missing,' said Ms. Harold. 'Fortunately we were at the dog beach. Immediately Sniff Detectives 2B and Maurice were at my side, using their noses to help in the search. I can't thank them enough!'

The ring was found partly buried inside a sand-castle tower but, with the tide beginning to rise, could have ultimately been washed out to sea if swift action had not been taken by 2B, the dog who found it. 2B and his canine co-worker Maurice are employed by Working Like a Dog, a sniff detection agency owned by Ms. Ginger Georges.

"2B, you really do have a twenty-four-karat nose."

Later I asked Maurice about that. "What does twenty-four-karat mean?"

"Twenty-four-karat gold is one hundred percent pure and extremely valuable," he answered. "Only the finest coins are made with it. I think this is a way of saying you have an extraordinary talent with sniffing. It is meant as a compliment."

Bow*wow*! No one had complimented me on anything much since Dragana and I had cooked together so long ago.

Ginger's phone started ringing nonstop. Business for all of us was exploding. We could have ended up being busy 24 hours a day. There were calls for lost wallets and glasses. Someone was desperate over a ball python that had slithered out of its enclosure. Usually we didn't accept these jobs. There were too many of them, and our noses were trained for bigger things, but there were a couple that we did take.

When Ginger answered her phone late one morning, a big booming voice filled the room.

"Ms. Georges? This is Commander Thomas Baird, retired US Navy, speaking. I've just read about your two sniff detectives on the internet and I'd like to hire them for a job."

"What do you have in mind, Commander Baird?" Ginger asked politely.

"I've lost my glass eyeball and I think your dogs can find it," he said bluntly. "I will pay handsomely for your services."

"I'm sorry . . . did you say eyeball?"

"I did indeed," he roared into the phone. "The dad-gum thing popped out when I sneezed. I'm sure it was the pepper in my seafood stew."

Ginger felt her own eyelid. Did she think this was some crazy joke? But she took the call seriously. "Commander Baird, where are you located?"

"I'm in berth eighty-one down at the marina," he responded. "Big, beautiful motor yacht."

"We can be there in about forty-five minutes," she said and hung up.

She looked at us. "OK, guys, you two have been specially requested for a curious assignment. It's on a boat, looking for a glass eye. Riot will stay here and hold down the fort."

I was sure Maurice, with his colorful history, must have known someone with a glass eyeball, but there was no time for his stories now. Ginger grabbed her van keys and we were off. Boats have always been uncomfortable for me because I tend to get seasick, so I was not looking forward to my time on Commander Baird's vessel. I just hoped I wouldn't lose my breakfast aboard.

The Bluefin

"**S**o good of you to come." A large, barrel-chested man with wiry white hair and a neatly trimmed beard, Commander Baird greeted us at the dock. "I've had to resort to wearing my eyepatch, so I probably look a bit like a pirate, eh?"

I could sympathize. I had once had an owner who dressed me up for Halloween as Blackbeard, and the eyepatch was the worst part of the whole costume.

"Welcome to the *Bluefin*, finest motor yacht of her class on the seas," he said, extending his hand.

"It's nice to meet you," Ginger said, shaking it. "This is 2B, and this is Maurice," she said, pointing to each of us in turn. I gave him a quick wag of my tail, as did Maurice. Then it was time for the unthinkable . . . crossing the gangplank. Ginger and Maurice strode over it with ease. Me? I stepped across tentatively, unsure of my balance. Where did I get this dislike of boats bobbing in water? I didn't know.

"Let me show you around," Commander Baird said. "Up there is the foredeck, aft is the captain's chair."

"Do you sail this by yourself?" Ginger asked him.

"Usually my wonderful wife Carole accompanies me, but right now she's trekking in the Himalayas with family."

"That sounds like quite an adventure!" Ginger said.

"I suppose," answered Commander Baird. "But I'm a sea dog at heart, much more comfortable on the water."

Well, there you go, I thought. *I'm definitely a land dog at heart.* I'd have to remember that line.

"I occasionally charter her out, so I do have passengers every now and again—I'm expecting some this afternoon and I didn't want to scare them off looking like a modern-day Jolly Roger. Let's go below."

Commander Baird went first and Ginger followed. They dropped down through a hatch in the deck and onto a set of stairs. Ginger guided Maurice, and I brought up the rear. That placed us directly in the galley, which is what sailors call the kitchen. Across from the galley was a navigation area with a computerized guidance system. There was also a dining table with some padded benches. There were staterooms for sleeping on both ends of the boat plus the smallest bathroom you could imagine. Commander Baird said it was called the head.

If you could describe fanciness in a thimble, this would be it. Everything you needed was here, just smaller and nailed down so it wouldn't go anywhere when the seas got rough.

"Commander Baird," Ginger began, "could you please describe the object we are searching for and where you were when you noticed it was gone."

"I am missing my right eye, and I have a glass eyeball as a replacement. The artificial eye was handmade in Germany by a highly skilled craftsman. It was created from white blown glass, with a black glass pupil, and a gray-blue-colored iris that matches my left eye," he answered with detail and precision. "It would be very difficult to replace it."

"And you discovered it was missing when?" Ginger prompted him.

"Earlier this morning. I was eating leftovers from last night's seafood stew out on the stern. The sunrise was spectacular. I shoveled in a large spoonful, and the spices really grabbed at my nose. I let forth with a horrendous sneeze . . . actually a series of three sneezes. I felt a pop and the eyeball was gone, like a billiard ball careening off the gunnels and the cabin wall. I've looked everywhere, but I can't find it."

"Well, Commander, that could certainly happen to anybody," said Ginger comfortingly. "Let's go back up on deck and begin our search there. Allow 2B and Maurice to roam freely." She pulled a marble out of her pocket. "This is the closest match I have to a glass eyeball, guys." We sniffed it and placed that smell in our memories.

We climbed back up the steps, out through the hatch, and aft to the captain's chair. There sat the bowl with remnants of the stew clinging to it. We inhaled that, encountering a cacophony of ingredients.

"I am betting the chili powder and pepper created the giant sneeze," Maurice said.

"Agreed," I answered, "plus maybe the garlic. I can imagine Commander Baird sniffing those nose-tickling spices, turning away from his bowl of stew, and letting it rip. *Aaachoo!* That eyeball could have richoceted off the back of the boat and . . . *plop!* . . . landed in the drink."

"Or it could have landed on the deck and rolled around somewhere," Maurice surmised. "It could be on the transom. I will search down there."

"First, let's get a better handle on what we're looking for," I suggested.

We both got close to Commander Baird.

"Sandalwood soap," I told Maurice.

"I am getting odors of earwax," he added.

"Leathery shampoo smell in the hair and eyebrows?" I asked.

"And blown glass," Maurice mentioned as he snuffled around Commander Baird's eyepatch.

"I concur. This may be a combo smell of glass, stew, sandalwood, and leather with just a touch of earwax."

"2B, when you describe the search in such full-flavored terms, it makes finding the object a simple matter. I doff my beret to you."

"You don't wear a beret, Maurice."

"I speak figuratively," he answered.

"Your dogs seem like they communicate with each other," remarked Commander Baird to Ginger.

"Yeah," she said. "They do share a deep bond."

I sat with my nose pointed up into the gentle sea breezes. Gulls wheeled and squawked, looking for food in the water. Maurice, true to his word, had already begun his ground game, sniffing along the transom, the lower deck where a winch was suspended above the back end of the boat.

"Could a seagull have swooped the eye out of the water and flown away with what it thought was a flavorful treat? Could it then have spit it out when it realized it had a glass eyeball?" I asked my friend and co-worker. "If so, where would the seagull drop it?"

Maurice looked up and said jokingly, "If it was a polite seagull, it would have deposited it in a trash can on the dock."

"Maurice, you're brilliant!" I took a flying leap off that boat and ran down the dock toward a can that was teeming with gulls. By the crowd around it, I guessed it would be here.

"Dumpster dive!" I barked, springing into it and scattering the angry, squawking birds.

"Yuck!" I gagged. Even for a dog, the odors inside were pretty ripe. Now all I had to do was filter out unimportant aromas like the really dirty diaper, the overripe banana, and yesterday's fish bait, and focus on our smell combo.

Was it here? I was betting that the gull in question would have flown over to the smelliest garbage can in search of a tastier morsel, trading the bland glass eyeball for something else. It would be hard to identify with so much foulness inside. I dove deeper and concentrated, driving my nose through layers of stink. *Bimp!* Wedged between a taco wrapper and a slimy mackerel head, my nose hit something small, round, and hard.

Coming up for air and wreathed in garbage, I tenderly held Commander Baird's glass eyeball in my mouth. "Eureka!" I woofed, which I think is Greek for *I found it!*

I scrambled out of the can and dashed back to the boat.

"Salty dogs!" exclaimed Commander Baird as I gently laid the eyeball at his feet. "He's found it!"

More like stinky dogs after being at the bottom of that trash can, I thought as he disappeared down the hatch. He reappeared a few minutes later with what looked like two normal eyes.

"Much better!" he said, smiling broadly.

Commander Baird was quite pleased with our work.

"Best money I ever spent—and entertaining to boot!" he thundered as he wrote Ginger a check to pay for our services. But before we left, Ginger tossed me overboard.

"P.U., 2B! That was a sweet search, but you stink! Rinse off a bit before we leave."

Maurice jumped in after me and together we dogpaddled around.

"This reminds me of the time Phillipe and I went swimming in the Mediterranean," Maurice puffed, his huge leathers floating on the surface. "We had been hiking on the Italian coast and jumped in to cool off. It was quite refreshing."

"You seem like you enjoy the ocean," I puffed back at him, remembering his doggy surfing at the beach.

"Phillipe and I swam in many bodies of water around the globe," he answered. "It was a hobby of ours."

Then we scrambled back onto the yacht's swimming platform and did vigorous body shakes.

"Great timing!" Commander Baird exclaimed as he walked us down the dock. "Here come my guests now."

Strolling toward us, I was surprised to discover that his passengers were none other than that unpleasant poohuahua I had once encountered at a dog show, being carried along by his owner, Amanda Puant.

We passed each other, they coming and we going.

"Grrr," snarled Tall Paul. "Surely that's not Snowball I smell. He looks more like Mud Splatter now but reeks of Garbage Dump. And, really, how can you stand to have your paws touch that dirty dock? I *never* set a paw on the ground if I can help it."

"Nice to smell you too, Tall Paul," I said.

"TP!" admonished his owner. "No growling!"

TP, I thought. *What an accurate nickname for that dog.*

Amanda had no idea she had seen me at the PoodlePalooza, but she did say, "Hey! He's the one that was on the internet. The sniff detective, right?"

We've met before, lady, I thought. *I was a finalist in that dog show. I do get around.*

Ginger stopped and smiled. "Yes, he is."

"Were you sniffing on the boats?" she asked nosily.

"Actually, we were exploring garbage cans," Ginger said, and then we were gone.

In the Treetops

As we were driving home, Ginger's frequently ringing phone rang again, and she answered it. "Hello, this is Working Like a Dog. Ginger Georges speaking."

"Help!" cried a youthful-sounding voice. "I'm trapped in a treehouse! Can you please help me find the key to get out? You and your dogs are my only hope."

"Perhaps you should contact the fire department," Ginger suggested kindly. "Have you called your mom?"

"I'm not a kid, and this isn't that kind of treehouse," came the response.

"Location?" asked Ginger. I could tell from her voice she was intrigued by the call.

It turned out it was on our way home, so we followed the directions given and pulled off the highway onto a dirt road. We bumped along until we arrived at an old barn. There were lots of trees surrounding it.

There was nowhere else to go, so Ginger got us out of the van to take a look around.

"Yo!" cried a voice from above. "Up here!"

Ginger looked up . . . way up.

"Why, hello," she called out. "You *are* in a treehouse!"

"I'm the cleaning lady. The owner is out and I've locked myself in up here."

"So how can my dogs and I help?" Ginger asked her.

The woman leaned over the edge of an outside porch that wrapped completely around a stately and very tall oak tree. Nestled among the branches was a small building that looked like a huge glass-and-metal birdcage some giant had hidden there. The strong limbs of the tree surrounded and supported the structure while the leaves hid much of it from view.

The lady was pointing down at a set of wooden stairs that canted out from the trunk to the ground. "Up here is a trapdoor that opens onto this porch," she explained. "It's essentially the front door. It closed accidentally, and it was locked. But I can't open it to climb down the stairs because I accidentally dropped the key on the ground somewhere. Thank you for answering my call. I read about you—"

"—on the internet." Ginger finished the sentence for her. "Seems like lots of folks did. Is it a regular key, or is there anything unusual about it?"

"It's a smallish, silver-colored key on a leather fob," the lady answered.

Ginger showed us her house key. "Sniff, pups."

This wasn't going to be as difficult as a ring at the beach or an eyeball in a garbage can, but there was a good bit of ground around the base of the tree, and it was littered with leaves, bark, branches, bugs, moss, and other forest flora.

"Maurice," I said. "As the Ground Hound, I defer to you. Give me some directions."

"Thank you, 2B," he answered. His nose went into vacuum cleaner mode, sucking up smells instead of dust. "Let us section off the area and each take a part. You start at the tree base and work left. I will go right and we will meet around the back side."

I sniffed in my direction, zigzagging left and right, while pawing up leaves and dirt near the wooden steps that led to the treehouse. I was quite thankful for this assignment. The scents acted like an air freshener for my sniffer, cleaning out the stinks from the boat dock. I was sensing almond and Froot Loops cereal aromas.

"*Ahrooo!*"

I knew that baying. It was Maurice, telling us he had located something.

I trotted back to him, and in his mouth was the leather fob, the key dangling by his chin.

"Good boy, Maurice!" Ginger praised him.

"We found it!" Ginger called up to the housekeeper. She climbed up the stairs, unlocked the trapdoor, and walked back down with the cleaning lady, who seemed to be quite relieved.

"Finally, my feet on terra firma," she said, and sighed. "How anyone can actually live in a tree is beyond me."

"Someone really lives up there?" Ginger asked curiously.

"Oh, yes. A woman and her prize-winning show dog," she answered, shaking her head. "It takes all kinds, doesn't it? How much do I owe you for this gallant rescue?"

"It's on the house," Ginger said. "Consider it our good deed for the day. We were heading home from another job so it wasn't even out of the way."

"Thank you so much," the lady said. "My name is Evelyn Martin. Here's my card if you ever need your house cleaned. I would be happy to return your good deed and clean it for free."

Debrief

"**N**ow that was a day!" Maurice exclaimed that evening after a bath and dinner. "I must say this line of work quite agrees with me!"

"Yeah," I said. "I'll sure miss you when you go home to Paris." I didn't want to think too much about Maurice's departure. It made me feel sad.

"How I wish I could be two dogs, one here and one there," Maurice answered.

"You found that missing key in a hurry," I said, hastily changing the subject. "*If* I wore a ball cap, I would tip it in your honor."

"Your compliment is graciously accepted," Maurice said with heartfelt sincerity. "But I discovered something else I feel is important."

"And that would be?" I asked.

"Do you remember the leaf smells under the treehouse?"

"I do," I answered. "They were a great nostril cleanser after the boat dock garbage. Scents of Froot Loops cereal and almond."

"Yes," agreed Maurice. "That would be the sassafras and the black cherry trees. But beyond one's natural interest in forestry, those were the very same scents I picked up at the library where the painting was stolen."

"Now that *is* important!" I exclaimed. "I remember your observations that afternoon. That was the day I had that bee sting on the old schnoz and couldn't smell a thing. I'd love to solve that case. What're you thinking?"

"Whoever stole that painting also walked near that treehouse, is what I am thinking," Maurice answered.

"But," I protested, "we were in the middle of the woods. There are bound to be trees like that everywhere."

"I disagree," Maurice said. "Believe it or not, we were near some of the trails where Sergio and I hiked when I lived with him. The black cherry is ubiquitous, but sassafras is much rarer."

"Ubiquitous?" I asked.

"It means it is found everywhere," answered my wise and well-educated friend.

"So, what you're telling me is that this particular smell combination is unique to this one spot," I responded.

"Exactly." Maurice nodded his head, and his leathers dipped and rose with the motion.

"If that's the case, then our thief is nearby," I surmised.

"Not necessarily," disagreed Maurice. "But they passed through there. Was it someone on a hike, a bicyclist pedaling through, or perhaps the lady who lives in the treehouse? I do not know yet, but I think with further investigation, we can figure this out. I believe we are scheduled to return to the police department soon to smell more evidence. Perhaps it will open new avenues of inquiry."

"I'm with you on this, *Inspector Maurice*," I answered as my friend stretched out by the fireplace.

We were enjoying the hospitality of Ginger's living room with Riot, spread out on the floor like a wall-to-wall carpet of dog.

"I don't know why we even have a kennel," Ginger said, shaking her head and smiling. "You three have almost completely moved in here. Where are our professional boundaries?"

But I could tell she loved having us around. I loved having us around too.

"This place is a dump!" she exclaimed. "We've all been way too busy . . . not that I'm complaining, but certain domestic duties have been severely ignored. I haven't washed the floors in days, let alone the windows. And don't get me started on the bathroom."

Ginger walked over to the table in the entryway and grabbed her backpack. She pulled out a business card and stared at it for a moment.

"Never in my life have I had a house cleaner. I've always been of the opinion that if you made a mess, you should be responsible for cleaning it up, but now that our business is finally taking off . . . maybe I will compromise my values on this and give Evelyn a call."

She reached for her phone and punched in the number on the card. Evelyn was happy to come the next morning, so Ginger got busy doing what many people tend to do before someone comes to clean. She started to tidy up her house. How funny humans can be!

Evelyn's Observations

Evelyn bustled in the next morning, her arms full of scrubbing supplies.

"Good morning!" greeted Ginger. "Would you like us to leave?"

"Heavens, no!" answered Evelyn. "I am quite capable of cleaning around anyone and anything. Just carry on with your work" . . . and she looked at us . . . "or sleeping."

Fine with us, too, I thought lazily. This was the first day off we had had in a while, and since we dogs usually sleep about twelve hours a day, I hoped to catch up on some lost winks.

"I'll start in the kitchen," Evelyn decided. She worked quietly and with purpose, scouring, sweeping, and polishing. She moved from one room to another, leaving everything behind in a much-improved state.

She thoughtfully cleaned out our dog dishes. She filled our drinking bowl with fresh water. She placed our toys back into the basket where they stayed when we weren't playing with them, and she hung up our security vests and dog leads. When she started vacuuming, she carefully worked around us.

"Seems like you have a fondness for dogs," Ginger commented, noticing how gently Evelyn moved among us.

"I owned seven of them over the years I was married," she answered. "When my husband passed and the last dog did too, I never replaced either of them. My kids are grown with families of their own. It's just me and my cottage now."

"Pretty quiet these days?" asked Ginger.

"Unlike my former life," Evelyn answered with a chuckle. "I was an undercover police officer."

That perked up my ears. Evelyn, a detective? Who knew? To me, she smelled like soap and furniture wax.

"Solving crimes is a risky business," Ginger said.

"It can be messy," Evelyn admitted. "Cleaning houses is much neater, at least when you're all done."

"Do you clean many houses?" Ginger asked her.

"Just one on a regular basis," Evelyn answered. "My neighbor is a young delivery truck driver. He recently started doing some home repairs for me so I've been cleaning his place in exchange. Plus, I take on a few other folks now and then."

"Like the lady in the treehouse?" Ginger asked.

"Oh, her!" Evelyn exclaimed. "Now that's a story all on its own."

"Really," remarked Ginger. I could tell by the way she said just that one word that she was curious about a human who would live in a tree.

By now Evelyn had grabbed her dust rag and was moving it methodically across the surfaces of the living room furniture. Riot was yip-yipping through a dog dream, her tail thumping madly on the floor while Maurice snored heavily.

But me? I may have had my eyes closed, but my ears were wide open. Who *did* choose to live in a tree?

"Yep," grunted Evelyn as she leaned down to wipe the baseboards. "You have to be a little off to live in a tree, in my humble opinion, even in a really fancy treehouse like that one. It's got everything you can imagine. Running water, electricity, glass walls to let in light.

"The woman who owns it seems nice enough, but I sure don't like her dog. That's one canine I can't warm up to. He's a show dog, and I know they can be temperamental and high strung, but he's off the charts."

"I think that kind of life can be hard on dogs," Ginger said. "Maybe that's why those two live in a tree. It's got to be peaceful up in the branches."

"I guess," Evelyn answered. "But they're often not there. They travel a lot. Like right now they're on an overnight cruise around some of the barrier islands. The funny thing is, this lady doesn't have any job that I can figure out. She just goes from one dog show to the next. Don't know where she gets the money for such a lifestyle. Maybe she inherited a bundle."

Evelyn went on with her cleaning, and Ginger went back to her work at the computer.

Wow, I thought. *A jewel from a collar like Tall Paul wore at the PoodlePalooza was in the library elevator, and it sounds like he and his owner live in that treehouse. Maurice will find this interesting.*

"All done," Evelyn announced sometime later.

"Thanks so much for coming," Ginger said. "The house hasn't sparkled like this in a long time. My business has really picked up recently, and I've let some things slide."

Evelyn nodded. "I'm glad you called me. It's been a pleasure to return a favor. Here's a little something for the pups." She handed Ginger a paper bag. "It's my own recipe. My dogs loved them."

Three dog noses started to twitch, and six eyes opened when Ginger peeked inside it.

"Chicken!" Riot said.

"With eggs and flax seed," added Maurice.

"I'm scenting garlic and sage," I put in.

"Covered with peanut butter?" asked Riot.

"What are we waiting for?" I wondered.

"An invitation, perhaps?" mentioned the ever-polite Maurice.

"Here, pups!" called Ginger. The three of us sprang up and hotfooted it into the kitchen.

"Sit!" she commanded, and three dog bottoms hit the deck. Three tongues hung out, and drool drips were starting to plop on the newly cleaned floor. Fortunately, before those drips could become a river, Ginger handed each of us a biscuit.

Heavenly!

They were gone before Evelyn was out the front door.

"They were well received!" Ginger called to her. Evelyn laughed and waved as she left. "Lucky pups! She gave us half a dozen so there're still three left for tomorrow."

Lucky pups indeed. You gotta love people who can bake like that for dogs. They definitely have insight into the canine palate.

Phone Calls

ring ding ding. Ginger's phone was ringing again. But this time it was the middle of the night.

"Hello?" she said sleepily. "What? Yes, this is Ginger Georges. You're calling from where? I can hardly understand you . . . oh, Tanzania?"

It had to be about Agnes and Irene and elephant poop. I had been in the light part of my sleep cycle and was instantly awake.

I heard Ginger say, "I'm so glad the research is going well! You need what? An extra dog and handler? . . . Can I come with Riot? . . . Yes, yes, I know. Science waits for no one. . . . I'd have to make arrangements here for two other dogs. . . . You need me there by Friday? . . . I'll see what I can do and get back to you. Bye."

"Phhooof!" Ginger let out a big sigh. "What do I do?" I heard her tossing and turning in her bedroom as I settled back down for the rest of the night.

The next morning, she made a flurry of phone calls, reaching out to those she knew in the sniff business or who loved dogs, but no one could take on Maurice and me.

She was in the middle of making scrambled eggs for herself when she said, "Why, how perfectly sensible and simple!" And she was on the phone one more time.

"Evelyn? This is Ginger Georges. How are you this morning? I'm glad I caught you. Listen, I got a call last night from Tanzania. . . . Yes, in Africa. I have two of my dogs there with a handler researching elephant herd migrations. But I need to fly out there with Riot to wrap up the research. I was wondering, would you be willing to housesit 2B and Maurice while I'm gone? They really seemed comfortable with you when you were over cleaning. I would be happy to pay you. . . . You would? Oh, thank you!"

Ginger immediately hopped onto the computer and made a flight reservation for herself and Riot.

Things heated up after that, with Ginger gathering gear for Riot and packing her own stuff. Evelyn came over for instructions and got a guided tour of the farm, kennels, and fields. The house she already knew, having just cleaned it.

"Don't worry about any of our outstanding cases or other sniff detection," Ginger said to Evelyn. "Just keep an eye on the Dognamic Duo over there," looking toward Maurice and me. "Feel free to take them out on hikes or let them roam the fields around the farm. They're very well trained and should be no problem."

"I've got your contact information, the name and address of the vet, and you're well stocked with dog food," responded Evelyn. "This should be a cinch."

"Let any messages for WLAD go onto the landline voicemail," Ginger instructed. "I've switched my greeting to that number. I don't think there's cell phone service out in the African savanna. On our way home, I've made arrangements to stop in London for the world-famous Bestminster Dog Show. I've always wanted to go, and timing with this trip works since we have to change planes in England anyway. We'll be back right after the show is over. Any other questions or concerns?"

"We should be fine, and you can always reach me by email if you're able. Otherwise, I'll assume that no news is good news."

And that was that.

The next morning, we waved our tails happily at Ginger and Riot by the curb of the departures terminal at the airport.

As we were driving home, Evelyn talked to us. "We're going to have a grand time together, guys. I'm of the opinion that free dogs are happy dogs, so you've got the run of the place. Just be back in time for dinner every evening."

Maurice and I couldn't disagree with that!

The phone was turning over onto the message machine as we walked in: "Merci, Ginger. Again, I'll be flying in for Maurice two weeks from next Thursday. I can't wait to see him and you again."

A punch in the stomach for me. That's the only way to describe how I was feeling. I loved where we were and what we were doing. Why couldn't it stay that way?

"It will be a sad day for me when I depart, but we should not dwell on it. We will make the most of our remaining time together, 2B," Maurice told me.

"Maybe Perline could be like her brother and move here," I suggested hopefully.

"I think not. She loves France. She always thought Phillipe was a little crazy to move away. In fact, I think she was upset that we left her to handle the restaurant in

Paris all by herself. Perhaps you should come to France with me."

I didn't know what to say. How can we have all that we want in one place? It never seemed to work out that way. Maurice would gain Perline and Paris. I would lose my best friend and a great co-worker. Crud. Crud. Crud.

"Maurice, let's get out of here before that phone rings again."

An Unnerving Encounter

We scratched at the door, and Evelyn let us out. "See you at chow time, guys!"

"Let us wander the farm," Maurice said. "I would like to officially deposit these scents in my memory. They will be a comfort when I am back in France."

"I'm all in, my friend," I said. "We don't have to be home until dinnertime. The rest of the day is ours. Sniff away." A few hours and many odors later, I stopped near the beehives.

"You know, Maurice, I've been thinking about our day in the library and that diamond you found in the elevator. Tall Paul's a show dog, and he had a collar with jewels like that. I overheard Evelyn tell Ginger that she cleans a treehouse for some rich lady and her show dog. Could they be Amanda and Tall Paul?"

"It makes sense," Maurice responded. "The scents in the library on the day the painting was stolen have been gnawing on my brain . . . especially the Chanel perfume. It is a custom blend made only for one individual."

"So let's check them all out," I said.

The treehouse was in sight when we noticed a human tromping our way. The aroma told us it was Amanda Puant. On her back was a small pack carrying Tall Paul.

Soon we stood facing each other near the old barn.

"The famous sniff detectives," Amanda said. "We seem to cross paths frequently."

Tall Paul growled.

"Yes, Stink-ums," she cooed. "These annoying dogs are everywhere, aren't they? Where do you think they're going now? Before we saw them at the dock, we saw them at the library the day the painting went missing."

The library? I thought. *This lady and her dog were at the library!* The smell puzzle pieces were coming together. I looked at Maurice. Our noses twitched at the same time. Amanda was giving off classic human fear odors: ammonia and vinegary scents.

She leaned toward me, her icy green eyes drilling into my chocolate-brown ones.

"So, keep your nose out of *my* business and *my* treehouse, Mr. Famous 2B. I have a recording that will put Ms. Ginger Georges in jail and land you in the city pound—not a place you'd ever want to be. Let me play it for you." Amanda held out her phone and pressed a button.

"Beautiful painting, isn't it?" It was Libby's voice in the library. And then we heard Ginger's answer.

"It's breathtaking. I'm going to take it home with me."

"Just in case you don't get it, I'll spell this out," Amanda said. "This is evidence that your owner was planning to steal that painting. I guess she did. The police would be very interested in this if I chose to share it with them. Don't make me. Now, shoo!"

She waved her hiking stick menacingly at us and turned on her heel, striding off down a trail, Tall Paul's growls fading in the distance. We hightailed into the woods, trying to hide in case she doubled back.

"That's all a lie," I choked. "Ginger didn't steal anything. She was admiring that painting and made a joke

148

about it. Amanda's the real thief! She stole that picture but left her smells behind, and we found them." But Amanda's threat had terrified me down to the tip of my tail. "Let's get out of here!"

"Absolutely not!" Maurice declared. "Ms. Puant has thrown down the gauntlet. We must defend our honor."

Gauntlet? Honor? All I knew was I didn't want to endanger my wonderful boss, my co-workers, or my job. Still, I needed to understand. "Explain, Maurice."

"In medieval times in France, men in suits of armor battled each other. If you wished for a fight, you would throw your metal glove, called a gauntlet, to the ground to indicate you were prepared to engage in combat."

"That's not something we need to do," I protested. "You'll be safely back in Paris while the rest of us clash with this crazy lady."

"All the more reason to find this painting soon and put this thief out of business!" exclaimed Maurice. "Let us proceed to Ms. Puant's treehouse and see what smells we may discover."

There was wisdom in Maurice's words. But did he *really* understand the risks we would face while he was vacuuming up crumbs in Perline's restaurant? Yet, I trusted him. So we ventured on, far from the safety of Ginger's farm and our caretaker Evelyn.

The Treehouse

Amanda's barn door was wide open. Inside, two men loaded a large, wooden crate in the back of a pickup truck.

"We just gotta nail it shut, Zeb," one man said to another.

"How about grabbing a bite to eat first?" Zeb answered. "I'm starving, and we've got plenty of time."

"Sure," he said. And the two men ambled out of the barn and around the corner.

This was when we hustled our tails, literally, inside for a sniff check.

"I think I smell the painting, 2B!" Maurice exclaimed.

"Are you sure? A barn is full of oily, brushy odors." The bee sting had left me with no scent memories of the robbery. I only knew about art smells from our training later on at the police department.

"Not exactly sure," he admitted. Then, nose down, he continued his snorting. He moved back and forth through the barn until he stopped by the crate that was standing open in the back of the pickup. "It is in here!"

There was a ramp from the ground to the bed of the truck. Maurice scampered up and into the crate. I was close behind. Underneath padded packing blankets, I could see part of a stainless-steel cabinet. It smelled like the show gear and supplies I'd seen all over the PoodlePalooza. There were also bags of kibble, pouches of treats, and jugs of distilled water stacked near a pile of comfy-looking dog beds and blankets.

"These two travel in style," I observed.

We both climbed over and around stuff, finally deciding to take a load off our paws and snuggle into the mound of pillowy pads. It felt good after all the walking we had done.

"A very odd fit!" Maurice observed, laying his front half in one bed and his hindquarters in another.

"Except for my legs, if I really squeeze in," I added as I tried folding my body up in another one, "I might be able to . . ." Before I could finish my thought, the two men had returned.

"Let's nail the crate shut and get on our way," Zeb said.

"Should we bark and let them know we're in here?" I whispered.

"No, 2B. We must stick with the painting. This is the best way to connect Ms. Puant to the robbery and ensure she will be securely locked away in prison."

Blam, blam, blam.

Maurice and I were now enclosed in our own prison. We could hear the engine being fired up, and the truck, with us, slowly drove away.

"I think this means we will not be home in time for dinner," Maurice said.

On the Road Again

The hours dragged on, and we kept motoring.

"Where do you think we are headed?" Maurice asked me.

"A dog show somewhere probably," I answered. "But why take a famous painting to a dog show?"

"Perhaps this is a sneaky way of sending it to someone without it being discovered," guessed Maurice.

"*We* just discovered it," I pointed out.

"Sadly, we are not in a position to tell anyone," Maurice answered. "We will have to wait and see where we end up. But thankfully there is water and food."

With his powerful jaws, he punctured a water jug and tore into the side of the kibble bag. We slurped and munched side by side in that very dark crate. It's a good thing we dogs can see with our noses.

"Better pickings than at that rest stop, eh, Maurice?" I asked.

"And that is fortunate," he answered. "The basset gas in here would be quite unpleasant."

He was right about that. Since there was nothing else to do, we fell asleep and I entered into a deep dog dream.

I am dog paddling through the air. "This is the only way to fly!" I think. The smells up here are clean and clear. I recognize so many: sassafras, honey, bees, and flowers. But there is another scent so powerful that it knocks my nose around in loops. What is it?

Maurice comes zipping by, his leathers flapping to keep him aloft, his tail spinning around in circles like a helicopter blade. "Do you smell it, 2B?" he asks me.

"Yes," I answer. "But what is it?"

"Quite simply, it is the smell of home," he answers. "I can make out the scents of love, care, loyalty, and protection, a four-smell combo!" And off he flies, his leathers and tail in a blur.

Now Maurice is starting to sound like me!

"Wait! Wait!" I bark after him. "Don't leave me behind! I want to find home too!" But Maurice is disappearing

and, as fast as I dog paddle, I feel like I'm now moving through mud.

"2B! Wake up!" Maurice nosed me in the side. "You have been yip-yipping in your sleep. Was it a bad dog dream?"

"It was a *strange* dog dream," I said.

Before I could explain it to him, we heard *floovb, floovb, vwomp, vwomp.*

Our truck slowed, and we could hear gravel crunching beneath us. Doors squeaked open and slammed shut.

And then a voice. "Great! A flat tire. Just what we need."

There was the clanking of tools, and the truck tilted to one side.

After a bit, the truck came back down to level again. "That's gonna cost us some time," one of the men said.

"Pedal to the metal," the other answered.

"Can't go very fast on that tire. It's low on air."

The truck pulled out onto the road again. Much later, it slowed and came to a stop.

We could hear different voices. "Hey, welcome to New York Harbor. You dudes are really late."

"We better get that crate on the ship ASAP!"

I groaned. "A ship? Please don't tell me we're going on a ship!"

"Is this a problem for you, 2B?" Maurice asked with concern.

"Yes!" I yelped loudly. "I get *seasick* very easily."

"Hey, did you hear a bark in that crate?" one of the outside voices asked.

"Huh? Let me look at the shipping label. It's going to England for the . . . Bestminster Dog Show. But there ain't no live animal sticker on it."

"OK," said another. "Let's get the crane down here to hoist 'er up. We'll get it secured once we're underway. This ship's ready to head to sea."

It was quite an experience to be lifted into the air. Maurice and I could feel ourselves swaying back and forth like the pendulum on an old clock.

"Waahh," I whimpered. "I'm feeling dizzy!"

"Stay lying down," Maurice advised. "We should not be swinging for too long. I remember the time Phillipe and I picked up a crate down at the docks. It contained a French stove for the bistro. Swinging back and forth, back and forth, it came off a huge iron vessel filled with many containers. They were piled up on the deck of a cargo ship like towers of blocks. It was a sight to behold."

Ugh. Piled up like a tower of blocks? This didn't sound like a great way to travel.

I decided to settle down and follow his directions. After a bit we felt a firm *thump!* and all was quiet.

Hhhnggghh. The ship's horn sounded a single, long, low blast. This announced its departure and ours as well.

At Sea

"Where's England, and how long do you think it'll take to get there?" I asked my well-traveled friend.

"England is across the Atlantic, 2B. It takes less than a day to fly across the ocean by plane, but a ship is much slower. I am guessing that it will take a week at least and perhaps more."

"I don't think we have enough food and water to last that long inside here," I told him.

"Ah, my apologies, 2B. My decision to remain with the painting may have been a poor one. But perhaps we can butt our way out."

We each took turns tackling one side of the box. When that didn't do anything, we both threw ourselves against it.

Skrzzutzz.

Our entire crate slid sideways and teetered slightly. But the wall we had tried to knock down stood fast.

"This isn't working," I told Maurice, "and I'm getting thirsty."

"Me, as well," he admitted. We treated ourselves to small gulps of water and lay down to reassess our situation.

"I could engage in classic basset baying to alert the crew to our unfortunate circumstances," Maurice volunteered.

"Have at it!" I exclaimed. "In fact, I'll join in with some yowls of my own."

The Cargo Ship Dog's Choir was quickly organized, and Maurice and I howled in harmony.

"*Ahrooo! Rowrff! Rowrff! Ahrooo! Rowrff! Rowrff!*"

We sang and sang. Sadly, our performance attracted no audience. No one heard us, and no one came to our rescue. Worn out, and with thirsty throats, we lay down in our beds and fell asleep. We slept and woke and slept and woke in what seemed like an unending cycle.

We were awakened from one nap by the sound of wind, rain, and crashing waves.

"A storm at sea," Maurice remarked.

"Huge seasickness for me," I moaned.

"Do you feel queasy?" he asked.

"Thankfully not yet."

"You may not get ill. Cargo ships are usually quite large, and therefore very stable in the water," Maurice informed me.

Ka-thunk!

It sounded like a massive wave had slapped the side of the ship. Our crate shook and wobbled and swayed.

"Bowwow!" I yelped. "That weather sounds pretty fierce out there."

"I am sure our ship will hold up in any storm," Maurice responded confidently.

I wished I had the same amount of faith in our vessel, but the wind, and now more waves, made me wonder. Could one of these things actually sink? I decided to ask Maurice what he thought about that when—

Ka-rack!

Thrack!

Tumblity-whack!

Swoosh!

Thunk.

It felt like Maurice and I were clothes inside a dryer, being tumbled over and over.

The next thing we knew, we were bobbing about in water.

"Dogs overboard!" I yowled. "Maurice! Maurice! Are you OK?"

"I am," came a dazed voice. "And our crate also appears to be in one piece. I can sense no water leaking in yet."

"Yet?" I asked, fear in my voice.

"Stay calm, 2B," Maurice said. "Stay calm." Then he added jovially, "You know, I do think that all the bedding padded our fall quite well."

There was wisdom in what Maurice said. I may have been bruised by the brutal crash, but we weren't cut up, and neither one of us appeared to have broken bones.

"We do seem to have some damage to the crate," Maurice observed as we spun about in the water. "A knothole was knocked clean out of one side so there is a small opening."

"Can it sink us?" I asked shakily.

"I think not," Maurice answered in his steady manner. "It is rather small. We must ride out this storm and see where the currents take us."

Sick as a Dog

The word *storm* did not describe what we were slam-bang in the middle of. Our crate flipped around and around. One second, up was down. The next second, left was right. The seasickness I had experienced on Bambi's sailboat was nothing compared to this. I threw up until my stomach was empty. And then I threw up some more. I was dizzy, and my guts felt like they had been yanked out of me and hung up on a clothesline to dry. My tongue was thick. My nose was dry. My eyes burned. I was thirsty, but even the thought of a drink made me shudder and spasm.

Maurice was concerned. "2B," he said. "Are you all right?"

"No-o-o-o," I howled. "So-o-o-o sick. . . . Sorry if you have barf all over you."

"Ah, do not worry, my friend," he said as we bounced around our ever-moving box. "One way or another, this too shall pass."

Eventually the waters calmed. The knothole was on the top of our wooden box. Sunlight beamed in. Some water had seeped inside, but considering our thrashing, it wasn't too bad.

"How are you, 2B?"

I weakly wagged my tail and croaked, "I'm still here. Sorry about the poop, pee, and barf. It's definitely an unwelcome smell combo."

"That was quite a ride," my friend remarked, politely ignoring my comment. "It reminded me of the time Phillipe and I traveled to Copenhagen. We visited Tivoli Gardens. It is Denmark's most amazing amusement park. The roller coaster there was our favorite. It actually had two giant loops where the cars would go upside down! Wheee! Loop the loop! We rode it over and over again."

Just hearing that made me want to throw up again, but I refused to vomit up nothing. "How come you never get dizzy or motion sickness?" I asked Maurice.

"I do not know, 2B. Movement has never bothered me."

"Lucky dog," I rasped. I was so wrung out that listening was about all I could do. Maurice's stories were always interesting, and I asked for another one. "Maurice, what are your earliest memories?"

"Of my family," he answered, "and of grapes. I was one of eight puppies. I have two brothers and five sisters. We were born in the village of Arbois. It is located in eastern France near the Swiss border. It is a place full of vineyards. We used to play hide-and-seek among the grape vines.

"Both my mother and father were French Grand Champion basset hounds. Three of my sisters and one brother were promised to owners as show dogs, but not me. I was a bit too plain for the ring.

"Phillipe had traveled to the area to purchase wine for his restaurant. On a lark, he peeked in on us at the winery. There we were, all snuggled up in a puppy pile. He plucked me out of the basket and cradled me in his hands.

"'Oh, little one,' he crooned. 'You remind me of a plump chocolate éclair!'

"We were smitten with each other on that first visit. Ten weeks later, I left with Phillipe and moved to Paris."

"Now, that's a classic puppyhood," I mumbled, starting to fade from consciousness. Maurice could hear this, and his question rallied me a little.

"How about you, 2B? Do you remember your earliest days?"

"Ummm," I answered unsteadily. It took all of my strength to speak. "I can certainly recall the warm, milky smell of my mother. I know there were other puppies, but I'm not sure how many of us were in the litter. I know nothing about my father. When I was just a few weeks old my mother ran off, leaving us behind. A kind woman found us in a culvert and took us to The BARC. It's a typical stray story, I guess."

Maurice was quiet for a moment. "A humble beginning for a dog as capable as you. You are making your mother proud, I think."

"I'm not sure we're making anyone proud, trapped in this crate," I answered weakly. "Evelyn must be frantic. We've let down Ginger who gave us so much training. We can't alert Officer M that we've found the painting. Perline will come to pick you up, but you won't be there."

"We are in a pickle, that is for sure," answered Maurice. "Perhaps we are headed for the Green Meadow, yes?"

"Land?" I asked hopefully.

"Not in the way you might imagine," he said sadly.

I waited for Maurice to continue, and he finally did.

"There is a beautiful grassy meadow where dogs go when their time on earth is finished. They play together, eat together, and do everything dogs love most. The Furry DogMother looks after them."

"She must have an awful lot of dogs to take care of," I said.

"They do not stay there forever," Maurice responded.

"Where do they go next?" I asked.

"They wait for their beloved humans to come and collect them. And together they cross the Rainbow Bridge to heaven. Phillipe is already waiting there for me. Perhaps Sergio is there too. I do not know what happened to him after the accident. But I do know it will be a joyful reunion."

I started to cry deep, heartfelt sobs.

"2B, what is wrong?" Maurice asked me gently.

"Who will I cross the Rainbow Bridge with? What happens to dogs like me?"

"Do you not understand, 2B? Both Phillipe and I will be there for you. As I said, it will be a joyful reunion."

"Thanks, Maurice," I whispered faintly, and I meant it from the bottom of my stray dog heart that had been broken so many times. Maurice had managed to glue some of it back together. In life, I think you need only one good friend. Maurice was my forever-friend.

By this time, we had been floating in our crate for several days. At least four. We knew this by counting the light and dark times. Our food and water were gone. We were low on energy and didn't talk much. We lay side by side on those beds and slept and slept and waited.

Pretty soon we no longer noticed the day and night. I felt as dry as an empty water bowl. Then everything went dark.

Awakening

Suddenly, a bright light made me squinch up my eyes. Fresh, clean air washed over me. The Green Meadow seemed like the best place to be after being trapped in that claustrophobic crate.

"Maurice?" I whimpered. "Are you here?"

"I am indeed, 2B," he replied.

I could make out his droopy-rimmed eyes, wrinkled forehead, big black nose, and enormous leathers leaning over me.

"We made it, Maurice," I babbled. "I'm ready to walk over the Rainbow Bridge. Did you find Phillipe?"

Maurice shook his head, his heavy leathers brushing my face. "No, 2B," he answered.

"How about Sergio?" I mumbled.

"No, 2B."

I was having a hard time wrapping my mind around all of this. "Where're all the other dogs and the Furry DogMother?" All I could see was Maurice's loving face and a blinding light all around him.

"They are not here," Maurice answered.

"So that was all a big fat lie?" I asked feebly.

"Au contraire, my true friend," Maurice said tenderly. "We will both travel to the Rainbow Bridge one day, but not this day."

"Huh?" I grunted.

"You almost decided to go without me," Maurice explained. "Commander Baird and I have been nursing you back to health."

"Commander Baird? You mean we didn't die and go to the Green Meadow? Don't tell me I'm back on a boat!" I moaned.

"You are indeed," Maurice said. "And we should both be grateful. We were plucked out of the water by the good commander, who was out cruising in the middle of the North Atlantic Ocean. You have been in and out of consciousness for several days."

Another face moved into my line of sight. "So, 2B, you've decided to join us? My friend, you had two paws in the grave and two on banana peels. We didn't think you would make it. Welcome back!" Commander Baird looked down into my face with his good eye and his glass eye. I was glad to see them both.

"I'm ready to hear another one of your stories, Maurice," I told him weakly. "This one is about two dogs bobbing around in the ocean."

"But of course, 2B. And as always, I will start at the beginning. After day four we were both unresponsive, perhaps deeply sleeping or maybe in a coma. Something latched onto the crate and I was jolted awake. It was the same feeling as when we were loaded onto the cargo ship."

"You mean swinging back and forth?" I asked.

"Yes," Maurice said. "There is a lift on this yacht. We were winched up out of the sea, and we landed with a clunk on the deck. I whimpered, and then I could hear someone prying off the crate lid. Imagine my surprise when I recognized Commander Baird! He was equally shocked to see us. The inside of the crate was quite disheveled. I was very weak but able to crawl out onto the deck."

"What about me?" I inquired.

"You were a different story. Not just weak, but gravely ill. Commander Baird radioed a veterinarian who has been advising him on how to treat you. It has been touch and go. But I think now you have definitely returned."

"I'm just glad we survived that storm," I murmured. "It'll be good to get back to Ginger's. The farm and the fields, even with those pesky bees, will make happy sniffs for homesick noses."

"But 2B," Maurice said, "we are not going back now. We are on our way to England."

"Why would we be going there?" I asked.

"I am not sure," he answered.

Cruising

grew stronger each day with the good care from Commander Baird and the good humor of my best friend Maurice. Pretty soon I felt like my old self again.

But Commander Baird shook his head. "2B," he said, "you look like you've been dragged through a hedge backward. There's no way I can comb out that tangled mess you call your coat. It's the clippers for you, mate."

Electric clippers were no problem for me. I'd survived looking like a bag of gigantic cotton balls at the PoodlePalooza. So once again . . . *BZZZZZ*. Clumps of matted fur floated away from me and out to sea. I wondered if they would line a seagull's nest somewhere. I was happy to contribute to the well-being of baby birds. I was immensely relieved that it was just my hair floating away and not me. Being without my coat made me feel lighter than air. I felt like I could fly.

Maurice was impressed with my new appearance. "My goodness, 2B. You look very different. I am not sure I would recognize you if I had not been here to witness your barbershop moment."

Commander Baird admired his work. "That's a regulation navy cut!" he chortled, stomping his foot for emphasis. "It looks mighty fine on you, sailor." Then he gathered his grooming tools and went below deck.

Ugh! *Sailor*. How had I gotten myself mixed up with a boat again?

"Do not look so disgruntled, 2B. We still have several days onboard before we reach our final destination. Relax and enjoy the cruise."

"I'll try," I said. "So, fill me in."

"I know very little," Maurice answered. "I have only heard Commander Baird speaking on the satellite phone. He described the contents of our crate to someone, and it was decided that he should sail to England to deliver it."

"What about us?" I wondered.

"We must continue to protect the painting," Maurice said resolutely.

"Where's it now?" I asked.

"It is in the belly of the dog stroller. However, no matter how I try to tell Commander Baird of its presence, he does not understand. Come, and I will show you."

On unsteady legs, I wobbled behind Maurice. How did he walk on a moving, uneven surface with such confidence?

"So, Maurice, do you have boating experience?"

"But of course, 2B," he said, turning back to look at me. "Phillipe had a small boat that we would take out on the River Seine. How lovely it was to glide underneath the stone arches of Pont Neuf, Paris's oldest bridge, on warm Sunday afternoons."

Maurice had a dreamy look in his eyes.

"Do you miss it?"

"It was a wonderful part of my life," he answered. "But I never imagined I would be sailing across the Atlantic with my forever-friend. Such grand adventures we have had together. Life brings many surprises, does it not?"

I had to agree with him. Who knew I would be cutting through the seas and not throwing up?

Maurice studied me. "Stand with your legs farther apart," he advised. "It will help you maintain your balance."

I paused on deck and tried it. I did feel more stable.

"See?" he said. "You are getting your sea legs already. Wonderful!"

Maurice led the way to the stairs that took us down below. Commander Baird was sitting on a chair studying his GPS monitor.

My basset friend sat in front of our commander. "*Ahrooo!*" he bayed.

Commander Baird looked up from his navigating. "What's up, sailor?"

Maurice climbed the stairs and walked to the crate. Commander Baird followed him.

"This again?" he asked. "There's something mighty interesting to you in there, so let's take another look."

Maurice led the way, and I followed. I hadn't been in here since we had been trapped, and I wasn't eager to re-enter. Maurice went over by the folded stroller, sat, and bayed again.

"We've been through this time and again, mate," the commander said kindly. "But no matter where I look, I can't find anything other than what we see." Then he turned and walked back to the helm.

"See," Maurice said. "I do not know how else to tell him of our discovery."

"I can understand your frustration," I responded. "But remember, he isn't trained in sniff detection." Then I cozied up to the underside of that stroller and sucked in a huge whiff of the painting to register it officially in my scent memory.

England

For the next two days, Maurice and I sunbathed, ate, and slept. It's the way of dogs, and we needed to gain strength after our horrific crate journey. We were lucky to be alive. I told myself this over and over.

Commander Baird had cleaned up the crate and nailed it closed in preparation for docking and delivery. The precious painting was still inside, and we had not figured out how to tell anyone.

"Land ho!" I heard Commander Baird bellow on the third day. "All dogs on deck!" Maurice and I hurried to the bow of the ship. That's what sailors call the front end. We stood side by side, legs planted firmly apart, and watched as the good commander guided our vessel into a berth.

After we had tied up the *Bluefin*, we off-loaded the crate. Commander Baird notified the harbor officials, and then we motored down the way to dock our boat.

Commander Baird punched in a few numbers on his phone. "We've arrived. The crate has been registered with the customs office and is in the delivery area next to some red metal cargo containers. We're tied up down the way with the other motor yachts." He listened for a few moments. "Aye, aye. We'll keep our eyes sharp for a white delivery van. See you soon." Then he hung up.

"Let's get our gear ready to go, boys," he said. "Our ride will be here soon." He went below and came back up with a duffel bag. He eyed us. "I guess you two don't need much besides yourselves." And he was right. We'd survived a great ordeal and having ourselves was enough.

We sat there in the early afternoon sun, soaking in the rays and feeling fit. I had to admit that being on this boat had been pretty nice. While we were lounging about, Commander Baird was scanning the area with his binoculars, looking for our ride. "Wait a second! What's this? A blue truck is picking up the crate. Are they trying to steal it? Not on my watch!" he suddenly roared.

He quickly opened a large hatch on the back end of the yacht and, using his high-powered winch, pulled up a small motorcycle with a sidecar. It sat squarely on the deck at the back of the boat.

"It pays to have wheels when you need to navigate on land. Hop in the life raft, sailors," he ordered, opening the sidecar door. We jumped in, and he strapped us down. Then he put on his helmet and revved that engine up near its limits. He did all of this swiftly and smoothly, as if he had done it hundreds of times before. With a pop of the clutch, he sent us rocketing forward, and we flew over the gap between the boat and the dock.

Thunk! The front wheel of the motorcycle hugged the wooden planks but the back tire was fighting to find its grip. *Vroom vroom!* He gunned the motor some more. We found traction and jetted out of the marina.

"We've got the wind at our backs now, sailors!" the commander cheered.

Maurice sat with me in the sidecar, stunned. That motorcycle had literally flown up off the *Bluefin,* over the water between it and the dock, and onto solid ground.

"It had to be my haircut," I told Maurice as we barreled along streets, keeping the truck with the crate in our line of sight.

"Pardon?" For once Maurice had little to say.

"My regulation navy cut made me lighter. I'm sure that helped us leap from ship to shore."

"I suppose that is as good an explanation as any," was all he said.

We sat together, letting the wind rush over us. It fortified us, and all of a sudden, this ride became the best one of our dog lives.

"*Yowlza!*" I howled as we zoomed onto the motorway. "I feel like a top dog! Can you catch all the smells?"

"It reminds me of riding with Sergio in his delivery truck, my head stuck out the window," he howled back. "He never minded letting me sniff the breezes." The wind whipped his leathers back, pinning them against his head. "I still miss him," Maurice said. "I hope he survived our accident."

We left the busy road and turned down a narrow lane. Our view was limited to leafy hedges on our right and left and a ribbon of gray asphalt spooling out ahead. We could still see the blue truck with the crate. Commander Baird was as capable at driving a motorcycle as he was at sailing a yacht until . . . he drifted over to the right lane of the road forgetting momentarily that people in England drive on the opposite side from Americans. A car was coming straight at us!

Honnnk! Screech! Honnnk!

"*Arrrooff!*" I howled in terror.

"Sacre bleu-hoo-hoo!" sobbed Maurice. "No! No! Not another crash!"

"Mayday! Mayday! SOS!" yelled Commander Baird as he violently jerked his handlebars back left. The other car zoomed by and was gone in an instant.

"A good reminder to stay vigilant!" he hollered at us above the wind. "We almost capsized back there!"

The road widened, and we picked up more traffic. The scenery changed, and we were now in a big city.

"London?" guessed Maurice. "I heard Phillipe mention this city from time to time. Other than the curry, he was not fond of their food."

Our speed slowed as the traffic thickened, but we could still make out the blue truck in the distance. We continued to follow as it turned into a large car park.

"Check out the sign," I said to Maurice. We could see a giant electronic billboard with pictures of dogs and trophies scrolling across it.

"The Bestminster Dog Show, I would wager," Maurice said.

It was at this point that Commander Baird turned around and motored away.

Hound's Hutch

"**W**e're entering safe harbor," the commander later informed us as we cruised into a small village. We turned down a long gravel drive. "This is the address I was given." At the end of it stood a large cottage with a thatched roof. Flowers grew in wild profusions around it. A white cargo van was parked on the drive.

As we were jumping out of the sidecar, the front door opened.

"We were worried about you!" said a familiar voice. It was Evelyn. Sheesh! Some people are so responsible, they'll travel halfway around the world to locate lost dogs!

She introduced herself to Commander Baird and looked down at us.

"It's so wonderful to see you both!" she said to me and Maurice. "I'd given you up as permanently lost." She bent down and enveloped us both in a group hug. But Maurice's eyes were elsewhere. A young man with a slight limp had followed her out the door.

"*Ahrooo!*" he bayed joyfully. "*Ahrooo! Ahrooo!*"

"What's up?" I asked him, somewhat confused.

"It is Sergio!" he answered, barreling toward the man like a miniature locomotive.

"Maurice!" I heard him call out.

The reunion between the two of them was heartwarming. They hugged and wriggled around. Well, Sergio did the hugging and Maurice did the wriggling, but you get the idea. If Sergio had a tail, it would have been a blur like Maurice's. Sergio may not have bayed any *Ahrooos*, but he actually did cry a bit.

"Oh, Maurice!" he said. "I've missed you, mi amigo. Looks like you survived the crash and some other adventures as well."

Maurice, for his part, could only lick Sergio with his big floppy tongue. But the licks were better than any words he might have spoken if he could have talked to people.

Now that's how it should be between a human and a dog, I thought. I was happy for Maurice. But I'll admit I did feel like the fifth wheel on a car, otherwise known as the spare tire. Where was my place with Maurice now that Sergio was back? Was he still my forever-friend?

"2B," Maurice called. "Come meet Sergio."

I walked over cautiously and gave him a sniff over. Nothing but good smells as far as I could tell.

Sergio gently put out his hand. "Hello, 2B. Evelyn told me you were Maurice's best buddy. Thank you for watching over him."

With those few kind words and that gesture, I knew immediately that Sergio was our kind of guy, a guy who understood dogs. Somehow we would all fit into this new puzzle picture together. I wasn't quite sure how yet. Time would tell, and I needed to be patient about it.

While we were checking out Sergio, Evelyn was ushering Commander Baird toward the front door.

"Let's not stand around outside," she said. "Welcome to Hounds' Hutch. I've rented the place for the whole week."

"Hounds' Hutch?" questioned Commander Baird.

Evelyn smiled. "Most older houses in England possess a name as well as address numbers. This building used to be a dog kennel for the lord of a nearby manor."

The commander frowned. "We're bunking down in a dog kennel?"

Evelyn laughed. "It's been updated considerably since it was first built several hundred years ago. I think you'll find it quite comfortable."

And Evelyn was right. Inside, everything was new and clean and designed for people. It looked like a regular house. But . . . Maurice and I could make out faint smells in the walls and wooden ceiling beams of hunting dogs from long ago. They were comforting and welcoming, like kindred spirits from the past. And, in a weird way, I felt like they were cheering us on in our own hunt, which we hoped was about to take place.

Interesting Observations

Evelyn, Sergio, and Commander Baird sat around the cozy dining room table drinking Twinings tea and eating chocolate digestive biscuits. Evelyn had even brought some of her delish-mo treats for me and Maurice. She was such a thoughtful dogsitter!

"Sorry to have missed you at the dock," Sergio said.

"The boys and I went on a short side trip," Commander Baird answered. "The crate they were trapped in was picked up by a blue truck. I wasn't sure what was going on so we followed it to the Bestminster Dog Show. The customs office called and told me they were able to locate the owner from a washed-out tracking number on the storm-scraped label. So it seems as if all is well."

"The most important part of the freight is safe and sound," Evelyn said, looking at us. "I'm so glad you called and left a voicemail for Ginger about the dogs. Now we're finally together again."

"It's great to see Maurice," Sergio chimed in, stroking the dog's leathers. "I had found him trotting along the side of Highway 27 the day after that dog shelter, The BARC, exploded. I picked him up and took him home. I figured he was a stray and his collar confirmed as much. He became my best buddy until we were sideswiped by an 18-wheeler while we were out on my delivery route. I was badly hurt and hospitalized for a while. I lost track of him after that."

"I'm glad you've recovered," Commander Baird told him. "As for these guys," he said, chucking us under our chins, "they do get around. Are you taking them back home soon?"

"Next week," Evelyn answered. "Sergio and I are neighbors, and Sergio was kind enough to accompany me on this trip. I thought four hands would be better than two when dealing with two dogs and international flights."

Sergio smiled. "I've never been to London before, so we'll do a bit of sightseeing over the next few days. How about you, Commander Baird?"

"I'll be hopping back onto the *Bluefin* and heading south to Portugal. Although I have to admit it will be lonely without these two onboard," he said, looking down at us fondly.

"Maurice can be a talkative pup," he went on. "He would go into the crate and bark and bark. If it had been me trapped inside that thing, I would never have wanted to go anywhere near it again. Yet, he kept going back into it over and over. I never could understand what he was trying to tell me. Was he afraid of it?"

Evelyn froze when she heard this. "Describe his behavior as accurately as you can," she asked the commander.

"Once he had gained his strength, and while I was nursing 2B back to health, Maurice would go into the crate, sit, then bark, then pause. He would wait for me to come over and look. He would do this many times each day. I would always go and check it out, but it was the same stuff."

Evelyn listened carefully. "Could you identify exactly what he was barking at?"

"It was some sort of stroller," he answered. "I even got it out and set it up for him. He kept barking and sitting by it."

Evelyn got out of her chair. "Please excuse me for a moment." She went into another room. Soon she returned.

"Commander Baird, you have just described the behavior of a sniff detective. I think Maurice was trying to tell you he had smelled something you needed to find."

"Finally!" Maurice said, slapping his tail on the floor. "They are understanding!"

"I've spoken with Officer M. He told me they had video of the library on the day the Mary Cassatt painting was stolen. It showed the back of a woman bending over a stroller."

Commander Baird stared at Evelyn. "I saw that picture at the library when I took my grandkids there! Could it be hidden somewhere inside that stroller?"

"I'll bet it is," she answered. "The dogs were at the library that day. I'm guessing they followed their noses and ended up getting shut into that crate."

"Makes sense," Sergio agreed. "From a smuggler's point of view, it's much easier to get valuables out of the country by shipping them overseas than to try and get them through airport detection."

"This means our sightseeing is canceled," Evelyn said. "We'll need to get 2B and Maurice to Bestminster to see if they can find that painting."

"If it's still there," Sergio added.

"The show doesn't start until tomorrow, so hopefully it is," Evelyn answered.

"I'll postpone my departure to Portugal to help in any way I can," offered Commander Baird. "I feel responsible for letting the painting slip away."

"But you didn't know how sniff detectives work," answered Evelyn. "I only know because of my police training and watching these two in action when they found a key I had misplaced." Then she went off to make another phone call.

Ginger Returns

"**M**aurice! 2B—is that you with a *haircut*?" It was early the next morning, and Ginger's voice echoed across the nearly empty baggage claim terminal. Three dog crates stood next to her.

And there was Riot greeting us from one of them. "Hey, hey, hey guys!" she panted. "Great to see you again. I've sniffed enough elephant poop to last me five dog lifetimes!"

Tiny beagle/shelty mix Agnes sat in her crate. Next to her, gentle giant German shepherd/Lab mix Irene waited patiently. They were both shy and remained silent. Sergio and Evelyn welcomed Ginger and they all began gathering up the mountains of gear we sniff detectives need for our work.

"Good timing," Ginger was saying to Evelyn. "We're ready to get over to the dog show. Who knew we'd be looking for the painting here."

"The sooner we start, the better our chances are of finding it," Evelyn said.

"And we know that the crate was delivered to the show grounds," Sergio added.

Ginger nodded. "It's a good starting point for dogs with 24-karat noses." She looked at me fondly. "Riot, 2B, and Maurice all have specific art theft training. We'll throw Agnes and Irene into the mix and do our best. Our first step is to get back to Hounds' Hutch and let the girls sniff Commander Baird and his belongings. There might be scent clues there that they can use."

We were passing by some baggage carousels when my nose went on high alert. It may not have been an explosive I scented, but it *was* something that I felt might blow me up. Wafting through the area was a delicate but distinctive aroma I had not smelled in a long time . . . orange creamsicle. I froze. Could it be Dragana?

A pretty woman with wavy dark-brown hair stood next to a carousel, waiting for her luggage. We were both older, and her hair, like mine, was shorter. But it was her. I was sure of it. What to do? I stood rooted to the floor near her while the rest of my group walked toward the elevators for the parking garage.

Predictably, it was my forever-friend who came to my rescue. Maurice sashayed toward me, sat, and bayed as loud as I had ever heard him.

"*Ahrooooo!*"

That got a lot of attention. Ginger hurried over, thinking Maurice was baying at Dragana.

"I'm sorry," she apologized. "My dogs are highly trained sniff detectives and one of them thinks he has smelled something of interest."

Dragana smiled her beautiful smile. "Perhaps it is the collection of Indian spices in my bag?" she asked. She opened it wide for us to see. "I'm a professional chef here in London, and spices like these are an essential part of my cooking. I've just arrived back from a trip to New Delhi."

Ginger grinned and shook her head. "Dogs and their noses," she said. "What can you do?"

"I once had a dog with an amazing nose when I was in culinary school, a big furry guy," Dragana responded. "In fact, I think his nose probably helped me become the chef I am today." She looked down sweetly at both Maurice and me. Then she turned, lifted her bag off the conveyor belt, and headed out through the double doors of the airport.

I was stunned. Numbly I followed Ginger and Maurice to the elevators. We climbed into the van and were off for Hounds' Hutch.

2B's Confession

"**T**hat was an interesting encounter," Maurice said to me as we drove along. We could hear Evelyn and Sergio filling in Ginger on what had happened since she and Riot had gone to Tanzania. The girls, tired after their hard work with elephants, slept soundly in the back.

When I didn't answer, he continued. "Those spices were nothing unusual. It was *your* odor that greatly worried me. Never have I smelled anything quite like it. I am thinking it was a mixture of deep despair and longing mixed with unrealistic hopes. Did I discover the scent of your greatest heartbreak?"

I sighed. It was time to fess up. "Do you remember, Maurice, back when we were residents at The BARC and you asked me what my greatest wish was?"

"I do," he answered. "You wished for a permanent one-way ticket out of the shelter."

"That wasn't the whole story," I confessed. "My full wish was to be with my first owner. The lady with the spices was that person."

"I have never heard you speak of her," Maurice said.

"She gave me away," I answered quietly, "and it broke my heart. I could never bring myself to tell anyone about her."

"And deep down inside you hoped she would come back?" Maurice asked gently.

"Something like that," I admitted.

Maurice stayed silent, thinking. Then he spoke. "We dogs do give our hearts to those we love. To be rejected is a most painful thing. Healing can take some time."

"Do our hearts ever fully heal?" I asked. "I remember you said you left part of your heart with Sergio. Phillipe must have also had a big piece of it."

"That is the wonderful thing about being a dog, 2B. We have such big hearts that a piece can be taken away and there is still more to share with others. That is the

heart of a dog. It is how we are made. We are always opti-
mistic, cheerful, full of love, and ready to serve."

Maurice's words made sense. The more I thought
about it, the more I understood I had just faced my greatest dream and my worst nightmare in a single moment.
And I had survived it. My heart was much bigger than I
had realized.

"And she gave you a huge compliment!" Maurice said
cheerfully. "I am sure she must carry a part of your heart
within her. Besides, your nose is far more than she could
ever use. Your nose will become legendary."

That Maurice! What a friend!

A Two-Smell Combo

"I haven't had so much attention since my grandkids' last visit!" protested Commander Baird happily. We were back at Hounds' Hutch, and the girls were filling their snouts with every scent surrounding the good commander. They scrutinized him, his clothes, shoes, pajamas, and, yes, even underwear and socks.

Ginger listened as Commander Baird shared his story of finding her sniff detectives in the middle of the Atlantic Ocean.

"2B and Maurice were in that crate for a very important reason," she said. "It has to be the painting. I'd bet the farm on it."

While the humans were talking, Maurice and I were fascinated by the observations of Riot, Agnes, and Irene.

"Mint toothpaste," Riot said.

"Laundry detergent," added Irene.

"Pigeon poop," noted Agnes.

"Pigeon poop?" asked Maurice. "On a boat out on the ocean?"

I agreed. "We didn't notice any birds in the crate with us."

"Or in the skies above us," added Maurice.

"They don't have to be there," Irene explained. "Their poop, or droppings, can be carried by many means."

"Such as?" inquired the ever-curious Maurice.

"In this case," she said, "it's on one of his gloves, just a faint scent of it. It might have been in the crate somewhere and he rubbed his hands over it."

"Hmmm," I said. "Like maybe smeared on the wheel of a stroller that ran through a plop of pigeon poop on a sidewalk somewhere?"

"Exactly!" agreed Irene. "2B, you are a pleasure to work with. You catch on quickly."

I gave a quick acceptance lick for such a fine compliment. "Thanks."

"So," Riot said, "we're looking for a two-smell combo: pigeon scat and oil paint."

"You are starting to sound like 2B," Maurice remarked.

"We can't help you with the second smell," Agnes chimed in, "but we're all over the pigeon poop scent, pronto."

"Show this smell to us," Maurice requested. "Then three of us can search for both."

We all went over to Commander Baird's duffel, and Irene nosed out the gloves.

"*Hmmf!*" wheezed Maurice. "It is a musty, sour scent, but now that you have pointed it out to me, I must say I have smelled it before. It was everywhere in Paris. I just did not know what it was."

"Did you wear these when you opened the stroller?" Ginger asked the commander.

"I did," he answered.

"Agnes and Irene have been trained primarily to scent animal droppings. By singling out your gloves, Irene is telling us there is a scat smell on them."

Commander Baird shrugged. "I only use them on the boat."

But we all knew. It was the faint smell of pigeon poop, hopefully our ticket to finding the painting, and, I hoped, saving ourselves from Amanda's threat to destroy us and WLAD.

Pahfff... wiff... pahfff... wiff. Out and in we exhaled and inhaled, planting that smell in our scent memories. Then our mutt meeting was over, and we were ready to move on out to the Bestminster Dog Show.

The Bestminster

"I say we divide and conquer," Ginger said as we were walking to the van.

"Meaning what?" Evelyn asked.

"Maurice and 2B know the smell of the painting. Riot has been trained to find art like it as well as poop scents, and Agnes and Irene know scat smells. How about two teams, with art and poop smellers in each?"

"Great idea!" Evelyn said. "Plus, we have an added bonus. Commander Baird, you have actually seen and touched this dog stroller."

"I have indeed," he answered. "I will keep a sailor's eye out and cover the grounds myself." He described the contraption to Ginger, Evelyn, and Sergio so they could also be on the lookout for it. "I'd like to stow my motorcycle in the back of the van in case I want to cover the grounds more quickly."

Sergio nodded. "I'll help you get it in."

Ginger studied our five eager dog faces. "Maurice, you go with Riot. 2B, you'll team up with Agnes and Irene."

We passed the same pictures on the big outdoor screen that we had seen the day before. The exhibition halls were huge, and everywhere there were dogs. I heard someone at the information booth say, "There are over two hundred breeds and fifteen thousand fine examples of them here this week. Welcome to the Bestminster!" Areas were roped off as show rings. This was like the PoodlePalooza but much grander in scale.

"I say we just let them have at it," Evelyn said. "They'll cover more ground without having to drag us along."

"Should we chance that?" Sergio wondered. "They got locked in a crate and landed in the middle of the Atlantic Ocean the last time they wandered off."

Ginger pulled something out of her pocket. "Trackers," she said with a smile. "We'll attach one to each dog's collar, and I can watch them on my phone. Then we'll know where they are. At the end of the day, we can all gather here at the entrance."

So we each got a new charm. The trackers were small round baubles that looked like dog bling. We all felt a little more fashionable and a lot safer wearing them.

Then, unclipping our leads, she said, "Pups, go find."

We knew what she meant, and we would do our doggonest to do just that. With wall-to-wall canines, it was easy to blend in here by ourselves to do sniff detection. And dog strollers were everywhere! The model in the crate was quite popular, and I noticed many of them wheeling here and there. And after pawing around the exhibition grounds for hours, I understood why dogs might like a ride.

In the later afternoon, Irene, Agnes, and I stopped by a fountain. We put our paws on the edge of it and lapped up a drink. "What do you think, 2B?" Agnes asked me, water streaming off her jowls. "Any suggestions? We've been over much of the grounds and the aroma of pigeon poop is everywhere."

"But no scents of oil paints," I added. "It's got to be a combo smell."

"But there have been plenty of other combo smells!" Irene said. "I'm partial to the fish and chips scents."

"Umm," I agreed. I was getting hungry. "How about if we mosey over to one of those food stands and see if there are any stray scraps lying around?"

There were plenty. So we did what comes naturally to us dogs, and we gobbled down everything even mildly edible. With full stomachs, we were better able to focus on our main task.

"OK, no more food smells," Irene told us. "Back to poop."

"That reminds me," I said. "How about a bathroom break? There's a pup poop place down there past those human ones."

"Lead on," said Agnes.

I showed them the way. We had just finished our doggy business and had rounded the corner of the human restrooms when we ran smack-dab into another stroller. It was parked by the entrance to the women's side of the building. In the interest of thorough sniff detection, we approached and cleared our nasal passages.

Pahfff. Pahfff. Pahfff.

Then we inhaled.

Wiff. Wiff. Wiff.

And we all agreed at the same moment that this time the smells had potential. I was smelling art odors and pigeon poop while the girls confirmed the second scent. Three bottoms sat and three sharp barks came out of three excited dog mouths, just as we had been trained. Sadly for us, there was no human handler here to take the next steps and run away with this contraption.

"We'll have to take matters into our own paws," I decided, "and fast, before the human who has been pushing this thing comes back."

"But how?" Irene asked. "We can't just stand up and walk away with it."

I thought back to the puskey racing I had been part of at the PoodlePalooza.

"We'll have to improvise," I said.

"Improvise?" asked Agnes. "What does that mean?"

"It means that I'm going to provide dog power underneath this contraption while you two guide me on either side of it." I squeezed partway underneath the frame. My head and front legs were wedged under the bottom of the stroller while my back legs and tail stuck up and out the back. I was just able to gain traction, and I started moving everything forward.

"You'll have to be my eyes," I told Agnes and Irene. "All I can see is the front bumper guard. Press in close on the right and left and stick to the sides like glue."

"Hey!" growled a grumpy voice from inside the stroller compartment. "Where are we going? Stop this instant!"

Had I heard that growl before? Maybe, but I was not in any position to stop for a yip or a yap right now.

The Great Stroller Escape

"**V**eer left!" Irene commanded.

I was thankful that Ginger had taught us our directions so well. We would need to use them accurately and smartly now.

"Right! Straight! Right again! Pronto!" Agnes directed.

We were starting to work as a team and I was impressed with these two. I hoped if we successfully solved this crime, we would have many more assignments together. I would even endure poop-smelling training to work with Agnes and Irene. They were impressive professionals.

"Left around the corner," Irene advised.

"Now straight." They told me later that we were quite a sight, a driverless vehicle in heavy traffic yet not running into anything. This was a miracle in its own right, considering how many people and dogs there were everywhere we went.

"Are we nearing the entrance?" I panted. I was getting hot and developing mild leg cramps from all the exertion. There was also the unending stream of barks and yowls from the passenger above me. I wasn't sure I could keep this up much longer.

"2B!" warned Irene. "Run faster! There's a lady chasing us!"

My blood ran cold. Was it Amanda? I turned on my afterburners, but there wasn't very much juice left in the old limbs.

Suddenly there was a powerful surge in the stroller and I slipped out of my command cockpit.

"Ahoy, mateys!" It was Commander Baird. "Full steam ahead!"

The dog upstairs continued to yowl.

"Pipe down, you scurvy cur!" Commander Baird ordered.

On we barreled, but I was no longer responsible for sailing this ship. I was merely a bystander. All I needed to do was trot alongside and keep up with Commander Baird.

"Give me my dog and stroller back!" yelled the lady. She wrenched the handlebars away from Commander Baird and quickly unzipped the passenger compartment. "Oh, Uttley!" she crooned, pulling out a black Scottie dog. "Are you hurt?"

Uttley took advantage of his owner's distress and whimpered pitifully. "You should be ashamed of yourself, taking my property!" she told Commander Baird angrily. "You've frightened my poor baby."

Commander Baird bowed slightly and said, "Madam, I do apologize. I mistook your stroller for another. It was not my intention to cause distress to you or your animal."

Then he straightened up and said, "That's a remarkably fine likeness of Uttley."

He was referring to an oil painting of the dog that was nestled inside the passenger compartment.

The lady seemed pleased by the compliment. "Thank you," she said, calming down. "I painted it myself. There's a dog art exhibition in a gallery nearby. I'm displaying Uttley's picture there. We're headed that way now." And she was off, cuddling her precious Uttley and giving the painting a comfortable ride to the gallery just across the road.

At this point, my nose went on crazy high alert. I could sense oil paint odors wafting out of that building, and I now realized they were all around us! There were many humans carrying paintings, milling about, all headed toward that gallery. If the stolen library painting was here, it would be nearly impossible to smell it.

We met up with Ginger, Evelyn, Sergio, Maurice, and Riot at the entrance to the show.

"A bust," I said to Maurice and Riot. "We thought we found it, but we were wrong."

"If I have to smell pigeon poop one more time, I think I will howl," Maurice grumped. "That aroma was everywhere. Sadly we scented nothing even close to our two-smell combo."

"We'll try again tomorrow," I answered, attempting to sound upbeat. But even I knew that finding this painting was a very tall order.

Car Park Discovery

"**O**K, everyone, back to the van," Sergio said. "It's on level one of the first car park tower. I'll run ahead and pay for the ticket."

While he hurried off, we trudged out of the dog show grounds. Everyone was tired and discouraged.

"I was so sure I had found it," Commander Baird remarked. He shared the story of Uttley and the mistaken stroller.

"You did your best," Ginger replied. "We all did, and you can't ask for more than that."

When we finally got to the car park, we spotted Sergio near the front of a long line of tired humans and dogs wanting to leave. There were crates, grooming tables, more strollers, and portable cabinets clogging the area around the payment kiosk.

"2B!" Maurice whispered urgently. "I am smelling the Chanel perfume that I scented in the library."

"Where?" I asked.

"It is very faint so I cannot tell exactly."

I lifted my nose and thought I caught the scent. Amanda Puant. My heart started to pound big-time.

"Please move your dog equipment away from the window," the parking attendant announced to the crowd. "And have your credit card ready to pay for your garage fee."

People were lugging things around while digging in their bags for those slim pieces of plastic that take the place of money. With all the confusion, I couldn't spot anyone who looked like our art thief.

"Maybe it's someone else wearing that perfume," I said.

"I think not. It is that custom blend," responded Maurice. "I have smelled many Chanel scents in Paris but this one is unique."

Finally Sergio was at the front. We could see him speaking with the lot attendant and slipping his card under the window.

"Thank you, sir. Deposit your ticket in the machine at the exit and the barrier will rise to let you out. Have a lovely evening."

Sergio waved us around the corner. He walked to the van, unlocked it, and slid open the side door. Commander Baird's small motorcycle was still tucked inside the back. Riot, Agnes, and Irene hopped in along with Evelyn and Commander Baird.

I was about to join them when I saw Maurice suddenly stiffen and stop. His large basset nose twitched. I recognized that movement. He had smelled something. At the far edge of the mound of canine show gear sat a dog stroller that looked exactly like the one containing the painting.

He quietly moved toward it, sniffed carefully, sat, and whispered *Ahroo* in the smallest basset bay I had ever heard. Fortunately Ginger heard it too. She tiptoed over to it, slid it away from the mass of stuff, and swiftly pushed that rig toward our crowded van.

"Let's get out of here!" Ginger exclaimed.

Things Go Sideways

Ginger ran toward the van with Maurice and me close on her heels. But it pays to watch where you're going. Unfortunately my long legs got tangled up in a heavily loaded equipment cart.

CRASH!

Then fingers grabbed my collar and jerked me away from my people and pack.

"Gotcha!" crowed a voice. But not just any voice. This voice was attached to that special Chanel scent Maurice and I had just smelled. Amanda. "We're going to swap property, you for the stroller."

She stuffed me into the slender passenger seat of a very sleek, cigar-shaped convertible. Slipping into the driver's seat, she turned on the engine and pulled out onto the car park exit lane. She was directly behind our white van. I could see Maurice's worried face looking out at me from the back window. Amanda bore down on our van, edging closer and closer until she was tapping the back bumper.

She's crashing into them! I thought. Sergio whipped the van into a vacant parking place while Amanda zipped by, furiously looking for a spot to stop. Glancing back, I saw that Sergio had reversed directions and was now climbing up higher into the tower.

"It's only one painting, although a very valuable one," Amanda told me as she too reversed directions, "but if I can't get it back, I'll keep you and that priceless nose of yours. You'd be very helpful to me in my line of work."

No way! I thought. *I would never sniff for a thief!*

It was a race up, Amanda's convertible trying to cut off the van. We twisted and turned, backed off and accelerated, always circling up and around that tall car park tower. My stomach was beginning to do a few twists and turns of its own.

Gaack! Urrp! Blaag!

Everything I had eaten at the dog show was making another appearance. Chunky dog barf sprayed all over Amanda, the steering wheel, and the windshield.

Bleck! Gaagg gaagg gaag! Round two came spewing out. This time it was gooey liquid. It landed in Amanda's lap.

"Gross!" she yelled, trying to turn my head away from her, but my whole face was a slobbery mess. Things got crazy after that with Amanda trying to grab the slippery steering wheel and me while trying to see through a barf-coated windshield. She lost control of the car and crunched into a cement post while our van disappeared around a curve.

There goes my ride, I thought sadly, *and everyone I love.*

But that didn't mean I was going to sit around moping. I took the opportunity to jump out of the passenger side of the car and run as fast as I could after the van. The last I saw of it, it had crashed through a guard rail, sailed into the air, and landed onto a connecting ramp of a second parking tower. *WHUMP!* The back door popped open and Commander Baird and his motorcycle roared out. I could see the dog stroller strapped in the sidecar.

now what?

Shelter dogs are resourceful. That means we take what we have and make the best of it. An approaching blue pickup truck was my best option. As it cruised down toward the exit, I jumped into the empty bed in the back and crouched down. At least it was a ride out of the garage. As it slowed at the exit gate, I bounded out and onto a frontage road. It was then and there that I knew Maurice's Furry DogMother was back in action and helping dogs on the down-and-out. Parked off to the side was our van with everyone, people and dogs, fanning out toward the parking structure.

"2B!"

I could hear Ginger's voice calling me. I galloped toward her and sprang into her arms. Bad decision. We both crashed to the ground, but she was laughing and crying at the same time while I was nuzzling her with my barfy muzzle. Everyone except Commander Baird was crowded around, cheering and barking.

"Hurry!" exclaimed Evelyn. "Get everyone in the van and let's get out of here!" We all jumped in and shot out onto the motorway.

"What a ride!" Evelyn exclaimed, as the van wound down the long driveway to Hounds' Hutch. We piled out, me on wobbly legs after all that dizzy driving.

"We've got some damage to the front fenders and bumper," said Sergio, examining the vehicle. "Either from plowing through the side railing or crashing through the exit gate."

"It's a rental and we've got insurance, so don't worry," said Evelyn. "Let's get inside and grab some grub. I'm starving!"

The humans sat around the dining room table eating, and we dogs lay on the floor after finishing our chow. As the shock of the car chase wore off, Ginger and Evelyn both started talking at once.

"Thank goodness we found 2B!"

"I'm amazed we're still in one piece!"

"Holy guacamole! That driver in the convertible was a maniac!"

"Flying off that ledge and sticking the landing! Where'd you learn to drive like that?"

Sergio sat back and smiled. "My dad was a Formula One race car driver back home in Argentina. I grew up at the track, and I've put in more than a few laps. My mom always said she was glad the bathtub didn't have wheels or I would have driven it out of the house."

Ginger looked at him. "If you can drive a delivery van like that, you've got the talent to be a race car driver too."

Sergio frowned. "Perhaps," he said quietly, "but my dad was badly injured in a race accident a few years back, and I promised my mom I wouldn't follow in his tire tracks."

"Well, thank you for your amazing driving today," Ginger said. "It probably saved us and the painting."

"Let's hope Commander Baird made it to his yacht," added Evelyn.

After a while, the conversation slowed, and everyone drifted off to their bedrooms. The house grew peacefully still. Maurice and I climbed the stairs to the landing, where we plopped down on some very comfy blankets.

"Those hunting hounds of yore are applauding you right now for smelling the painting," I said to Maurice. I was referring to the scents and spirits of the dogs who had lived here hundreds of years before.

"And you, as well, 2B. Your vomit prevented Ms. Puant from crashing into the van and doing real damage."

"We're a team, Maurice, and we each do our own part. Amanda scares the fur off my ears, so we still need to get her, or she'll get us."

"Do not worry, my dear chum," was all he said before he drifted off to sleep.

Chum? I thought. Maurice certainly had unique ways of calling me a friend.

Remarkably, I didn't feel tired yet. I guess it was all the adrenaline from the chase and the escape.

It was a good time for me to think. I was amazed at where my life had taken me. The explosion at The BARC had been a big turning point for me, that and meeting Maurice, of course. What a difference having a friend made. I could not have been more grateful to Ginger for taking a chance on me and training me as a sniff detective. It was a relief to know that my heart was bigger than Dragana. My life seemed to have acquired some purpose and direction.

Almost perfect, I thought. *If we can just lock up that crazy lady. . . .* I turned around in a circle a few times and fell asleep.

Homeward Bound

Commander Baird called early the next morning to say the painting was in a secret compartment inside the stroller. To celebrate, we took a romp in St. James Park: 58 acres of grass, trees, and ponds. It reminded me of home, and I was eager to get back. We stayed a few more days, enjoying the sights and smells of London.

Ginger had spoken with Perline on her phone. Perline would be arriving at the farm the day after we got back. Then Maurice would become a memory.

The night before we left was a blur of activity as we packed for our departure. But I remained apart from it, retreating to the upstairs of Hounds' Hutch and saying my final goodbyes to the spirits and smells of those ancient hunting dogs.

"We hunted our best here," I told them. "And I promise to make you all proud by continuing to hunt well when I go home." I was a sniff detective, and I wanted to sniff my heart out for the rest of my time on this earth.

I had never flown before, but the team assured me we would be fine. After all, these were dogs with travel savvy. They had jetted around the world. It turned out to be a regular dog motel in the hold with all of us lined up next to each other. Agnes, Irene, and Riot settled down immediately. Maurice's crate was next to mine and we chatted through our wire windows.

"A most memorable trip, yes, 2B?"

"It's been quite an adventure," I answered.

"There will be more such adventures for you in the future," he assured me.

"I'll be sorry not to share them with you," I said. "You told me back when we were truffle hunting that we made an excellent pair. You were right. We were a great team."

"We still are, 2B. We are a forever-team."

And with that powerful and comforting comment from my forever-friend, I settled down for the journey.

If you've ever been cramped in a small space for eight hours, you'll understand what a relief it is to straighten out. After transfers in New York and Charlotte, we landed in Jacksonville. It took a while to unload the baggage and crates, but Ginger, Evelyn, and Sergio were there with smiling faces to let us all out. The airport was very dog-friendly. It had a pet area where we canines could catch some fresh air and rub our backs in soft grass.

After that, we hopped into a couple of taxis and headed back to the farm. We spent the remainder of the day wandering the fields and keeping out of the way of the bees. It was the dog days of summer again. So much had changed in one year.

That evening we all gathered for dinner. Ginger had pizza delivered, and Sergio and Evelyn stayed for the meal. There was much laughter and talking.

"Could you believe all the dogs at the Bestminster?" Ginger said. "That's a lot of noses sniffing the breezes."

Evelyn smiled and nodded. "It was an unexpected treat to have visited there. I still can't get over how two dogs in a crate in the ocean led us to the painting in England."

"Those few days in London were an experience I'll never forget," added Sergio. He especially loved Commander Baird's escape from the back of the van.

"Vroom-vroom," he said. "I can still hear that motor-cycle engine, jetting down the connecting ramp . . ."

While he was speaking, we heard the *vroom-vroom* of a real motorcycle outside, and a booming voice blew in through the screen door.

"Ahoy, mates! Welcome home to us all!"

"Commander Baird!" exclaimed Ginger. "How are you?"

"I'm a bit worse for the wear, actually," he said. "It was a beast of a trip back. Storm season, you know."

Maurice and I looked at each other. We knew what could happen when big waves slapped at the sides of your ship.

"I skirted the worst of it, but it did slow me down. I just made port this afternoon and headed straight here, after one errand along the route."

"And the painting?" Evelyn asked eagerly.

Hidden Discoveries

"I'll need a screwdriver," Commander Baird said.

Ginger went to fetch one, while Commander Baird unloaded the stroller from his sidecar. He also carried in a small canvas ditty bag.

"Check this out," he said, emptying it. *Clunk!* A diamond necklace thudded onto the table. "This was around the dog's neck."

"Good grief!" exclaimed Evelyn. "That looks like something the Queen of England would wear!"

Commander Baird then unfolded the stroller. Maurice's nose twitched in that familiar way, as he nuzzled its underside.

223

With everyone gathered around, Evelyn removed the padding from the inside bottom of the carrier and unscrewed a panel.

"Ohhhh!" Huge gasps filled the air. There, nestled down in the space, was the beautiful painting we had seen when we were reading companion dogs at the library.

"I thought it was best to leave the evidence as I found it," Commander Baird explained.

"Good idea," agreed Evelyn. "The police will know what to do."

Evelyn immediately called Officer M. You could hear him whooping through the phone. "We'll come and get it right now. And I'll call the owners and give them the good news!"

While we waited for the police to arrive, Commander Baird pulled up a chair and grabbed some pizza. As he ate, he filled us in on what had happened after he left us.

"I drove down that ramp and out of the garage as slick as an iceboat on a frozen lake, sped down the motorway and got to the docks, no problem. After loading up my motorcycle, I set sail. The seas were quite rough. I couldn't decide what was worse . . . the wind howling, or that little runt of a mutt I found in the stroller yowling. He had a temper more foul than Neptune's."

"Roman god of the sea," Maurice whispered to me.

The commander paused to take another bite and a swig of root beer. Then he continued.

"Fortunately, I knew how to handle the pip-squeak. He and his owner had chartered my yacht for an overnight outing around the barrier islands earlier in the year, so I had seen him in action before."

"How *did* you handle him?" Ginger asked curiously.

"I just kept stuffing food down him. I will say he gained a few pounds on the voyage, though." The commander laughed. "When I dropped him off at his point of destination earlier today, he reminded me of a tiny version of the Goodyear Blimp with legs."

"Well, at least we helped by getting the painting back," Evelyn remarked. "The police can figure out the rest of this case."

"Oh, for the love of dogs!" I exclaimed, slapping my tail on the floor. "These humans aren't getting it. Amanda Puant stole that picture. It's as plain as the nose on my face." We dogs were lying together under the dining room table.

"Yes, 2B," Maurice said. "It is as plain as the noses on all of our faces. Sadly, humans cannot smell like we can. That means we have until I leave tomorrow morning to show them."

"Let's go get this lady, pronto," Agnes said.

Nighttime Raid

We immediately scratched at the door. Ginger opened it and we all burst outside in a blur of focused dog fur.

"I am pleased we are on our way," Maurice said. "But what exactly is the plan when we arrive at Ms. Puant's residence?"

"We found the painting, Tall Paul is long gone, and the police have the stroller," I explained as we sprinted toward the treehouse. "We need to find just one more piece of evidence to nail this lady."

"The collar with the missing jewel!" Maurice exclaimed.

"You're reading my mind," I told him.

"2B, since you possess the 24-karat nose, I suggest you be the designated diamond detector," Maurice said. "Let us handle Ms. Puant."

Irene, Agnes, and Riot wagged their tails in agreement.

When we got there, only a single light glowed from the upper level of the treehouse.

"Who wants to stay here to try and lure Amanda out of that oversize birdcage?" I asked.

"I volunteer," said Maurice. "I have an eerie howl she will wish to investigate."

"I'll stay on the ground as well," Riot said.

"Me, too," added Irene. I looked at Agnes. "That means you and I are going up."

"Pronto!" she cheered.

We scampered up the steps. The trapdoor was down. I pushed hard with my nose, and it opened enough for Agnes to squeeze through. Sadly I was too big to wriggle in.

"Let me know what you find," I said to her.

"Will do," she answered, and then she was gone.

"Agent Agnes is on the porch," I reported to the rest of the team after returning to the ground. We were hidden among trees and bushes near the base of the huge oak tree.

"Roger that," Riot said.

"*A-h-h-h-r-o-o-o.*" Maurice bayed a bone-chilling howl. Riot added some forlorn barks of her own while Irene produced an undertone of menacing growls. It sounded like ghost dogs in a graveyard. More lights went on in the treehouse. A glass door opened and a human stepped out onto the porch. The smell was unmistakable: Amanda Puant.

A fiery ball of fur exploded on her ankles. It was brave Agnes.

"We've got her," I said.

"OUCH! I've been bitten!" screamed Amanda. She grabbed that swirling mass of beagle/shelty and tossed it over the porch rail. Agnes landed on a branch of the majestic oak, scrabbling to stay on.

Amanda opened the trapdoor to escape while we charged up the stairs. Jackpot! Irene burst through the opening first and flattened our thief. Amanda popped up and limped back inside her house. But we were hot on her heels. Up, up, up a sleek spiral staircase we all dashed. It felt like we were on a caffeinated elevator.

Finally we were on the top floor of the house. It looked like Amanda's office. At one end sat a large modern desk and a high-tech roller chair. Tall shelves lined one wall, decorated with a few books, some vases, and a small statue of some guy's head. A high-tech wide-screen TV was mounted on a stand in the middle of the room.

"She's cornered now!" I howled. But Amanda Puant dodged our snapping jaws and sprang onto the roller chair, which, true to its name, rolled at high speed across the room. *CRASH!* She and her chair slammed directly into what might have been the world's most expensive television.

The chair spun out of control and rammed into the the stairway. Amanda jumped up onto the steps, racing toward the ceiling. She struggled for a moment, trying to open the latch to a rooftop patio door.

"Ugh, ugh," she grunted. "It's stuck!"

She swung out over the railing, grabbed the statue off its shelf, and hurled it through a nearby skylight. The glass shattered. Then she pulled herself up and clambered through the sharp, jagged opening.

I led our team up the stairs, took a ginormous leap off the highest step, and sailed through the broken window after her. We stood facing each other on a tiny rooftop patio. A huge, NASA-size telescope loomed between us. Amanda swiveled the optical tube in my direction. I ducked under it and lunged at her. Dodging me, she quickly attached a harness around her waist and flung herself off the glass-paned roof, into the darkness.

Impressive! I thought. *She's done all this with a decent bite in her ankle, courtesy of Agnes.* I hoped Agnes was still holding onto that branch.

"Zipline!" I barked down to everyone. "She's escaped!"

"Was that a bust of Napoleon that Ms. Puant heaved through the skylight?" Maurice called up. "No matter.

We will charge after her, just as Napoleon charged at the Battle of Austerlitz. My French nose will miss nothing."

"We're with you," Riot and Irene chorused together.

The three streaked down the stairs like there was a tub of juicy steaks calling their names. If any dogs could find Amanda, it was them.

OK, Wonder Nose, I told myself. *Find that collar.* I tried to think of all the places a human might keep such an item. It could be wherever she stored dog stuff. It wasn't in this room. I trotted down to the second level of the treehouse. My nose told me this was a bedroom and bath. No sign of dog stuff here either.

The first floor was the kitchen, dining room, and a pantry. Poking my nose inside the pantry, I could smell stale kibble, treats, and fancy show shampoo. There was a pile of old blankets and a dog coat. On a hook in the wall were leads and collars—lots of them. I nosed them off and pawed through them. An acidic carbony smell led me to the collar I had seen Tall Paul wear at the PoodlePalooza, the one with a missing diamond.

Eureka! I thought. *I found it!* Grabbing it in my teeth, I hurried out of the treehouse, and down to the ground.

"2B, help!" yelped Agnes. "I'm slipping!"

I looked up. It was at that moment that I saw some branches break and heard a heavy thud. It was Agent Agnes, her body motionless on the leaf-strewn ground.

Rescue

sprinted over to Agnes. She didn't move when I gently nudged her. But she was breathing. What to do? I couldn't move her, and the rest of the team was gone. I decided doggy first aid was my best choice. I lay down and curled my body around my friend and co-worker to keep her warm.

"It's not time for you to travel to the Green Meadow," I whispered in her ear. "We'll all be there someday but not this day." Worried and tired, I drifted into a light sleep.

I jerked my head up later at the sound of sirens blaring. Lights flashed and humans jumped out of a police car, running toward us.

"The missing police dogs have been found!" Officer M announced.

"Phew! I'm relieved the trackers still work!" It was Ginger's voice. And then a huge gasp. "Agnes?" She bent over and examined the small dog. "Her paws are chilled. She could be in shock."

Officer M was close behind. "It looks like she's out cold. I'm calling immediately for a backup car. They'll take you straight to the emergency vet."

Impatiently I grabbed Officer M by his shirt sleeve and tugged. The collar that had been clenched in my teeth fell at his feet. *We need to find the team and help them*, I urged. *There's no time to waste.*

"What's this?" he asked, examining it. He turned to Ginger. "I'll bet my badge a certain diamond fits in this collar."

"Yes, but where are the other dogs?" Ginger asked, worry in her voice. "2B, can you find them? Do you need human help?" Even though time was short, I answered her questions by sitting and barking once as I had been trained.

"Here's my phone," Ginger said to the policeman. "These blue dots on the GPS map show where the rest of the pack is. Take it and 2B and see if you can locate them. We can communicate through the police channel while I get Agnes to the vet."

Between my 24-karat nose and modern tracker technology, Officer M and I were off. He held a bright light out in front so it was easy to go fast. I could smell my co-workers, Chanel perfume, and a light scent of blood. On and on we hiked. Sometimes we zigged left or zagged right. We stopped every so often to look at the phone dots.

"They're off in three directions," Officer M told me. "Which way should we go?"

But I understood hunting and figured one of my co-workers was trying to lure our thief one way while two other dogs circled around to close in. So I started off in the direction with the strongest two-smell combo of perfume and blood.

"Now the dots are bunched together. Come on, 2B. This way."

We broke into a run, crashing through bushes, tripping over roots and rocks, and dodging tree trunks. There in a clearing was Irene, sitting atop a struggling Amanda Puant while Maurice and Riot growled menacingly.

"Perfect timing, 2B," Maurice said through a mouth of seriously sharp-looking teeth. "We have restrained Ms. Puant. Law enforcement protection is greatly appreciated."

"Police," Officer M announced to Amanda and my three teammates.

"Thank goodness," Amanda responded. "I'm being savagely attacked by these crazy mutts. They entered my home, bit me, and chased me clear across the county. I'm going to sue them."

"Good luck with that. I don't think you can sue dogs. Right now, I'm taking you in for questioning about the robbery of the library painting." Then he expertly snapped handcuffs on her.

"What?" she squawked. "This is false arrest! I'll have your job for this."

Office M calmly led the captured thief back to the tree-house, calling for another police car. When it arrived, two officers jumped out and put the struggling Amanda Puant into the back seat. They drove away while Officer M and we four dogs jumped into his car. It was a short ride back to the farm, where Evelyn greeted us with a solemn face.

"I heard from Ginger," she told Officer M. "Agnes has a mild concussion and a broken front leg. I'm taking all the dogs inside the house and staying the night."

He nodded, waved, and drove away while we went in and got water, biscuits, and blankets to sleep on. Then Evelyn turned off the lights and headed to bed herself.

"It has been a magnificent night for us sniff detectives, with the exception of Agnes's injuries," Maurice began. "And as my last night on the job, I am proud we have wrapped up this case."

That made my heart sink. I'd momentarily forgotten that Maurice was leaving for Paris the very next day.

Bon Voyage, Maurice

Morning came way too soon, and with it came Perline. She drove up in a shiny rental convertible and eagerly hopped out. Maurice and I greeted her at the door along with Riot and Irene.

"Maurice!" squealed Perline. She grabbed him up in her arms and hugged him closely. Maurice wagged his tail and licked her face, but I wondered if he was really sincere. He was such a polite dog with everyone.

"We're so glad you made it here safely," Ginger said. She too was being polite, I thought. She would miss

Maurice almost as much as I would. "Can you come in for a cup of coffee?"

Perline looked at her watch. "I am afraid we must get going. It will take longer to check in at the airport with an animal, so I want to allow for extra time." To her credit, she did lean down and pat me gently on the head. "Hello, 2B. We meet again. You are always invited to travel to Paris to visit your friend Maurice. We would both love that."

It was a kind comment, and I was grateful for it. Maurice and I looked at each other.

Pahffff.

Pahffff.

We both exhaled at the same time and then . . .

Wiff.

Wiff.

We officially sniffed in the aromas of each other. It would be a lasting memory, for we sniff detectives never forget a scent. Maurice might be leaving, but I would always have his smell, and he mine.

"Goodbye, my forever-friend," he said. "Remember, being left behind can also be the beginning of going on. And please wish Agnes a speedy recovery for me."

I gave him a lick. "Goodbye," I whimpered. It was all I could say.

The car drove away, and I could see Maurice's leathers flapping in the breeze.

It was quiet for a moment, and then Ginger said, "2B, let's you and I head to the vet. We can pick up Agnes."

Yes, I thought. *Let's bring Agnes home.*

We stopped at the same emergency veterinary practice where Maurice had been stitched up after his accident with Sergio. So many memories. I was glad to have them. These were memories I wanted to keep in my head, unlike many of my earlier ones when no one wanted me.

"Hello, 2B," murmured Agnes as Ginger gently wrapped her in a blanket. "It's good to see you. You'll have to fill me in on our adventure last night. I conked out partway through."

"Sure," I snuffled at her. "I'll tell you all about it when you've rested up a bit."

We made our way through a group of humans on the lawn outside the vet hospital. It was a local animal rescue group. They had set up some wire pens with dogs inside them. Signs were attached to the enclosures. Ginger read them as we passed by. "Dogs are everyone's best friends. Please let me be yours. Adopt."

"Dwayne! Come look at this one." It was a voice from my past. I stopped and saw Doreen bending over one of the cages. "Isn't he cute? I could do up his hair real nice, and he wouldn't take up much room in the rig."

Dwayne shrugged like he always did and said, "Sure, let's get him."

In her arms was a dog I recognized by smell. He looked quite different from the last time I had actually seen him. He was much chubbier. But there was no mistaking that foul growl of his, and he never missed a chance to use it.

"Snowball again?" he snarled as we brushed by him. "Our paths keep crossing. Who gave you such an uninspiring haircut? It doesn't do much for you . . ."

His insults faded away as Doreen and Dwayne headed for one of the volunteers and we walked toward the van. I wondered if my second-place ribbon was still in Dwayne's coat pocket, but it wasn't important anymore. I had moved on to better things.

Putting on the Dog

The leaves on the trees were glowing golds and reds. There was a nip in the air. Agnes was healing up and eager to get back to work. Thankfully Amanda Puant had not been able to convince a judge and jury that Ginger or we dogs had harmed her or lent a paw in stealing the library painting. Last we heard, she was headed for prison.

We were busy, busy dogs. I learned to scent scat. Poop smells weren't my all-time favorite, but I figured the more scents I had, the better I would be at my job. I was with Riot on this one. We were born to work. Along with

Agnes and Irene, we made a great team. We filled four of the five runs in our kennel. Maybe Ginger would find one more good sniffer to give us a full house.

We had heard from Perline. She and Maurice were safely back in Paris, and he was getting back into the swing of being a restaurant dog. I could imagine the tidbits that were falling on the floor in that place! It reminded me of my early days with Dragana. I didn't miss her anymore, and I was thankful that she had loved me when I was a puppy. I'm sure it gave me a good start in life.

One day Ginger pulled a large, fancy envelope out of the mailbox. "Check this out, pups!" she said to us after she had opened it and read the card inside. "We've all been invited to an awards ceremony hosted by the owners of the stolen painting. They want to reward us for our work! We've been instructed to *Put on the Dog*. That means we must dress in our fanciest clothes."

We were all groomed and wore our WLAD collars and security vests. We even had our teeth brushed. There's much to be said for chicken-flavored toothpaste. It's totally delish-mo!

Evelyn, Sergio, and Commander Baird had also received invitations. Commander Baird dressed in his navy whites and looked like a true officer. His wife Carole was back from the Himalayas, and she came along too.

Sergio rented a tuxedo, and Evelyn wore a beaded gown. Ginger went out and bought a new dress for the occasion.

The event was held at a fancy downtown hotel where canines would not usually be allowed, but this was our night and we were all greeted warmly. There were many people there.

"Welcome! Welcome!" The police chief and the mayor hailed us.

"Your places are at the table up front," said the maître d', escorting us through a large dining room.

"We're sitting *at* the table?" I asked. "Like *on* chairs with our bowls *on* the table?"

"Let your hair down a bit, 2B," Riot told me. "It's our big night."

"Do I smell rare roast beef?" Irene asked.

"I hope there's lots of gravy with it," added Agnes.

"There is!" I exclaimed, seeing waiters bringing us our chow in silver bowls.

We ate heartily and accepted seconds gratefully. All in all, it was a meal extraordinaire, as Maurice might have said if he had been there.

The awards ceremony was to follow the dinner. But first, we had to wait through dessert. Dogs can't eat chocolate. Unfortunately it's really bad for us. Thankfully Evelyn provided each of us with one of her amazing dog biscuits. It was the perfect end to that perfect meal.

Finally everyone settled down with coffee or tea, and the speeches began.

"Ladies, gentlemen, and dogs, welcome!" said the mayor. "We are here this evening to celebrate the talents of sniff detection and to raise money to rebuild The BARC, a caring canine adoption center. All the dogs you see here this evening lived in shelters at one time or another in their lives. They have been rescued and retrained to lead productive and helpful lives."

Such kind and true words, I thought. The speeches droned on and on. I decided to spend the time analyzing the smells in the room. *Pahffff. Pahffff.* I blew air out of my nasal slits, closed my eyes, and delicately inhaled. *Wiff.*

Hmmm, I thought. *I'm sensing chrysanthemums, hazelnuts, candle wax, a slight whiff of basset gas . . . basset gas?*

Wild applause snapped me back to the room, and walking toward me was Maurice!

"Huh?" I gasped. "Maurice?"

"Airplane food, 2B," he said, knowing full well I had smelled that stink. "It was the dog biscuits. They were nowhere near as good as Evelyn's. We got stuck in traffic so we are a tad late. I must say the private jet we traveled on is the only way to fly! I had my own leather seat with a comfortable blanket. Can you imagine?"

My head was spinning, but I was now well enough trained to stay in control. Maurice and I could jump around after the event. Each of us was awarded a medal that was draped over our heads. Ginger received one of those huge cardboard checks for $10,000.00. It was enough to bring tears to her eyes. Pledges poured in to rebuild The BARC. All in all, it was a night to remember.

"2B, why don't you ride back to the farm with Maurice?" Ginger suggested at the close of the festivities. "He and Perline will be staying with us for a few days."

We hopped in the back of a long black car.

"Only you, Maurice, could figure out how to score a limo ride!" I told him.

"Well," he said, "the invitation was difficult to refuse. The owners of the painting flew us here. It was very generous of them."

"It's good to see you again, old buddy," I slobbered, tears welling up in my eyes.

"And you as well, dear friend," he answered.

"So, how's Paris working out for you?"

"Jet lag," he answered, yawning widely. "I will tell you all about it tomorrow."

A Brilliant Idea

The next day dawned bright and clear. We were up early, romping around in the farm fields with the girls.

"Up for a hike?" we asked Maurice.

"But of course," he answered. "Sadly I am not in the same strong physical condition I once was, but I should be fine. It is far too easy a life I lead in the restaurant."

"So what's a typical day there like for you?" I asked as we headed out into the trees.

"Flaky croissants and cold cuts for breakfast, then a nap, a leisurely stroll along Parisian boulevards, more napping, catching restaurant morsels that fall to the floor, dinner, and sleepy evenings by a fire," he answered.

"Bow*wow!*" I exclaimed. "And here I've been learning poop smells. Sounds like you got the better deal."

Maurice was uncharacteristically quiet. "I am not certain of that, 2B," he finally said. "Although I am fond of Perline, my heart no longer desires to be in Paris. I found great purpose here with all of you. Being a sniff detective is a noble calling, and I felt we accomplished much."

"So stay here," Agnes urged him.

"Yeah," said Riot. "Your kennel run is still available."

"You're part of our pack," Irene reminded him.

"This is our home," I pointed out. It sounded a little strange to my ears, but we *were* home. All of us.

Maurice shook his heavy leathers from side to side. "There is no way I can communicate this to Perline. I am afraid my fate is sealed. But I will never forget our adventures together. And I will always hold a special place in my heart for Sergio. He rescued me from the side of a highway. He is such a nice man."

"Maurice," I said, "I'm determined to figure out how you can stay."

"Thank you, 2B," he answered. "If any dog can do this, it is you."

We hiked along, and I thought and thought. There up ahead was the old barn and the treehouse. They both looked abandoned. The wall-to-ceiling windows on the treehouse were coated in dust.

"Memories," said Agnes, looking up at the tall branches of the oak.

"It was a successful raid," Riot remarked.

"Our last full team effort," Irene mentioned.

"At least Ms. Puant is paying her debt to society," added Maurice.

"Tall Paul is too," I told him.

"How so?" asked my forever-friend.

I told him what I had seen outside the vet hospital.

"An appropriate end for *that* churlish canine," Maurice said. "I hope WLAD will have many new and exciting sniff adventures."

"I'm sure we will," I answered confidently. "Our business is exploding."

"*Your* business," corrected Maurice sadly. "I will be far away in France, sniffing and sitting only for crumbs."

An idea hit me then with such force, I felt like I might have been knocked flat by a Greyhound bus. "Maurice," I said, changing the subject, "how often did you try to tell Commander Baird about the location of the painting?"

"Hmm," he said. "Many times a day, 2B. But he did not understand. It was not his fault. Sniff, sit, bark. He did not know what that meant."

"I'm thinking we're looking at a two-smell combo," I told him excitedly. "Or," I added, "it could be a single smell."

Maurice cocked his head. "I am not sure I am following your thinking, my friend."

"Come on, fellow sniff detectives," I exclaimed, running back toward the farm. "We've got the most important assignment of our lives coming up right now!"

Determined Dogs

We ran full tilt toward home. Agnes, with her stiff front leg, and stubby-limbed Maurice lagged behind, but we waited for them. We neared our kennel, empty now because it was daytime. I moved next to Maurice's old run.

"Go inside," I instructed him. He did. Then I pointed my nose in the air, sniffed, sat, and barked once. Riot repeated this several times until she and I got the attention of Ginger and Perline. Agnes and Irene joined in and took turns sniffing, sitting, and barking as well. It was a total team effort.

"Maurice, go outside of your old run," I urged him.
"Then put your nose down near the entrance, sniff, sit,
and bay."

Which he did.

"Do it again," I ordered him.

Which he did. Over and over again.

By this time, Ginger and Perline were standing near
all of us.

"What's up, pups?" Ginger asked us. Then she explained to Perline, "They're displaying classic sniff detection discovery behavior. In other words, they've found something very important."

They searched and searched but came up empty-handed. "I don't know what's gotten into these dogs," Ginger said, shaking her head. Then they walked back to the house.

"What have we discovered, 2B?" Maurice asked me.

"Your true home," I answered. "We've found you *and* your scent inside the run, and you've found your run."

"But Ginger knows where I stayed," Maurice protested.

"True," I answered, "but now we are telling her in the clearest way we can that this is where you *live*. Staying somewhere is temporary. *Living* somewhere is permanent. Trust me, I should know." The girls wagged their tails, showing they knew too.

The light went on in Maurice's droopy-rimmed eyes. "Ah! You all are detecting the two-smell combo: Maurice and the kennel. I am indicating the single smell: my run. Brilliant, 2B!"

We were all on the same page now. It was only a matter of repetition. For three solid days, we did nothing but sniff, sit, and bark, over and over. Yes, it was boring and tiresome, but the team was doggedly determined to give this our all.

Unfortunately, Ginger and Perline were still confused. But, we didn't give up. The fourth day began like the previous three. This time, Ginger sat in a folding chair out by our kennel and watched and thought. This was a human who truly wanted to understand what we were trying to communicate. I loved that about her.

I could see her thinking. Then a lightbulb went on in her head. She stood and called us all over to her. Of course we obeyed.

"Pups," she said. "I think I've figured this out. Dogs, you are showing me the discovery of a fabulous sniff detective named Maurice, who lives in this kennel run. Maurice, you are showing me where you, the sniff detective in question, live. Am I correct?"

We all immediately sat, and barked. It was our sign that we had found something. This time, it was Ginger's understanding. She got that too.

She laughed. "I'll go share this with Perline. The final decision is hers."

A serious discussion followed. We lay crowded under the table listening in. In the end, Perline agreed to leave Maurice with WLAD.

"He will certainly be more stimulated here, I think," she said. "The restaurant life is a little slow for a dog of such adventure. And he will have loving care. Will you promise me visiting privileges?"

"You can see him anytime. We can also come to Paris. I've never been there before," Ginger answered.

"I think Phillipe would approve." Then Perline bent over and rubbed our ears. "You all are a pack of very determined dogs!"

I had to agree. Maurice, Riot, Agnes, and Irene determined. And . . . me, 2B, determined.

We were finally home, all of us.

Author's Note

Sniff detection dogs are busy every day helping humans around the world. They are highly trained and eager workers who use their noses in search of wild animal scat, bed bugs, cancer, people buried by earthquakes or avalanches, illegal drugs, bombs, and contraband such as exotic animals or fish. You might see them at airports, or with search and rescue teams like firefighters, the military, or police.

They have a very strong drive to work so they usually make poor pets. Because of this, their humans often neglect them or give them away. Frequently these dogs live in shelters or are found wandering the streets of towns alone. It's a good thing that organizations and trainers are on the lookout for these amazing dogs everywhere. When one is found and has no owner, it is admitted to rigorous training programs and sent out into the field to help keep our world safer.

If you would like to learn more about these incredible canines, here are a few books and websites to explore:

AKC Detection Dog Task Force • akc.org/akc-detection-dog-task-force

The Marshall Legacy Institute • marshall-legacy.org

National Disaster Search Dog Foundation • searchdogfoundation.org

Nationalgeographic.com "Detection Dogs: Learning to Pass the Sniff Test" • nationalgeographic.com/animals /article/detection-dogs-learning-to-pass-the-sniff-test

Nationalgeographic.com "These sniffer dogs are learning to smell the coronavirus" • nationalgeographic.com /animals/article/see-dogs-trained-to-sniff-covid

National Narcotic Detector Dog Association • nndda.org

Poop Detectives: Working Dogs in the Field by Ginger Wadsworth

Sniffer Dogs: How Dogs (and Their Noses) Save the World by Nancy Castaldo

Traffic.org Wildlife Sniffer Dogs • traffic.org/what-we-do/projects-and-approaches /wildlife-conservation-technology/wildlife-sniffer-dogs

I'm Pearl (aka The Chocolate Puddle). I'm a big, beautiful Gordon setter, and I've got the best human in the entire world: Cindy Neuschwander. We live on the California Central Coast. That means we go to the beach where I get to run and dig. We also hike and take walks together.

Cindy often goes away during the day. She usually comes back smelling like little kids and school. Other days, she smells like the grocery store, the swimming pool, or church. When she's home, she sits at her computer and writes stories and reads them out loud to me. Cindy's written a lot of books, but *2B Determined* is her newest one. She's more excited about it than a dog trapped in a meat market!

So . . . stick your nose into *2B Determined* and get reading!

Emily Tetri is a visual development artist for animation and a children's graphic novel author and artist. She lives in Los Angeles, California, with her fiancée and their pack of animals.